THE WON
ROUNDABOUT

STORIES FOR KIDS AND OTHER SMARTY PANTS

Mandy Olina

Discover new, wonderful stories weekly at:
www.wonderfulroundabout.com

Book illustrations and cover design by Șerban Gabriel.
www.serbangabriel.com

To my extended family of lovable smarty pants, who have made the roundabout wonderful.

TABLE OF CONTENTS

THE ROUNDABOUT OF FRIENDS AND FRIENDSHIPS

THE MOUSE WHO LOVED HIS BICYCLE

Part I

'Mouse! You don't look yourself today. Is something the matter?'

'I'm hungry. I couldn't find anything to eat today. Nobody leaves anything outside the fridge anymore. I'm starving.'

'Oh, Mouse! I'm so sorry. Want me to recite a poem to you?'

'Yes, Topsy. Please let me hear a poem.'

'Once there was a tree,
Who wanted to be a bee.
And every time he went to sleep
He dreamed he went off his feet;

Flying high above grass
Like a turtle in a glass.'

'Topsy that's wonderful! It makes no sense whatsoever.'

'Lovely, isn't it?'

'It is. You are.'

'Oh, Mouse!'

'I wish you had feet and we could travel the world together.'

'Well we do travel the world together.'

'Only when Maria takes you out and I climb into the basket. I'm sure she can see me in there, but I think she likes it.'

'Of course she does Mouse, you're adorable.'

'No I am not. I am a silly, powerless mouse who loves your poems. But you know what? Nora the blackbird told me a secret. She said that she heard of a witch who can turn anything into anything. So I was thinking...'

'You were thinking about turning me into a mouse?'

'Well, not necessarily a mouse. Almost any other walking, reasonable creature would do.'

'Are you tired of visiting me, Mouse?'

'Of course not, Topsy. I just want to do what's best for us. I want us to be together all the time.'

'So what else did that Nora hear about the witch?'

'That she lives in an old, run down house up the hill, by the river fall.'

'Oh, she's living in that creepy old house between the walnut trees, isn't she?'

'Yes she is. And I was thinking of visiting her.'

'Oh, Mouse, but do you think she'll turn me into a mouse just to do us a favor?'

'I don't know, Topsy. But whatever she wants me to get her, I'm going to get it. I want us to be a happy family of mice.'

'Oh, Mouse! You are an unbelievable creature.'

'Topsy, I can hear footsteps. I think it's Maria. If she takes you out I'm coming into town with you so I can go talk to the witch.'

'Quick, climb in!'

As soon as Mouse tucked himself under a pink scarf, a little girl came into the room eating a giant peanut butter and jelly sandwich.

'Oh, yum! Peanut butter! I love peanut butter crumbs!' Mouse thought.

Maria climbed on the bike and placed the remaining half of her sandwich in the basket for safe keeping. She then pedaled to the gate and out of the yard.

'What luck!' Mouse thought. 'She's heading straight up the hill. Walking over there would have taken me at least a couple of hours. I can almost smell the breeze of the river fall.'

'Topsy! We're almost there.'

3

'I know, Mouse, but Maria always makes a left at the next intersection, you know that. You're going to have to jump off and carry on by yourself. I wish I could come with you. I hate leaving you alone.'

'Don't worry, Topsy. Just slow Maria down so I can jump safely and afterwards I'll take care of everything!'

'Please be careful. If the witch puts you in danger just run away and come back home. I couldn't stand losing you!'

'You won't lose me, Topsy. I'll be careful and I'll get the witch to help us!'

'We're almost there. Climb down my fork, and I'll shake my chain off so Maria has to stop.'

'I love you, Topsy!'

'I love you, Mouse!'

THE MOUSE WHO LOVED HIS BICYCLE

Part II

The mouse ran to the witch's house as fast as he could. He was sure she'd say yes. After all, why wouldn't she help them? There was no harm in it.

He dashed through a grove of walnut trees until he was nearly at the witch's front door. When he was almost at the door, a ray of sunlight bounced off of the silver door knob and the reflection blinded him. He stopped confounded for a second and raised a paw to his forehead.

'What? What is that? Oh... oh, no. No, it can't be! Aaaaaaah!' Mouse yelled and started running as quickly as possible, back towards the walnut trees. He reached a little burrow under one of the roots just in time.

'You can hide, little white mouse. But you can't hide forever. I know you're not from around here. When you decide to leave, I'll be right here waiting.'

'I have no business with you! I'm here to see your master!' Mouse said bravely. 'I have something to ask of her!'

'Do you know what my master does with little white mice? She saves them a nice cozy spot... in her jars of magical ingredients! I want to catch you first, so I can eat you before she rips you apart!'

'Oh, dear me,' the mouse thought to himself. 'What on earth am I going to do?! I promised Topsy we'll be together. How am I ever going to get out of here alive, let alone help us? I'm a silly, silly mouse. What was I thinking? Why didn't I ask if she had a cat... I'll be here for hours!'

The hours went by, just like that. The cat watched outside the burrow and Mouse stayed huddled and worried inside. When the sun started to set, Mouse convinced himself to make a run for it. His chances were not good, but he couldn't stay trapped there forever, either. So he thought up a plan and found the courage inside himself to just go for it. Mouse waited for the cat to turn its back for an instant. As soon as he saw its back, he jumped out of the burrow and ran as quickly as he could towards the gate.

Now this is where a bit of real magic happens. When the cat saw the little white spot of fur moving quickly through the grass, it wasn't bothered. 'The little squirt actually had the courage to run away,' he thought. Pretty brave for a mouse. Most of them just waited around until they almost fainted with hunger and then became easy targets. But not this one. This mouse was either really determined or just plain crazy. So the cat, being a curious animal as you may expect, suddenly called:

'Waaaait! I'm not going to eat you. I promise. Please stop! I want to talk to you!'

The mouse couldn't make out the first few words so he just kept running for his life. The cat raced after him but couldn't catch up with him before he got to the street.

'Well I'll be. That's a fast, determined little mouse,' the cat thought. 'I have to talk to him. I'll follow him, he must live close. I'll just wait for him outside his house and then he'll listen to me.'

Mouse ran all the way home, crawled right under the wall of the shed and right into Topsy's basket. She was asleep.
'Topsy! Please wake up, Topsy! Oh, I missed you. I thought I was never going to see you again!'

'Mouse... what did you say? I'm awake. Please say that again.'

'Topsy, I got so close to the witch's house when...' And then he stopped. If he told the truth, she'd never let him leave again.

'When what, Mouse?'

'When I... tripped on a twig and fell in the river. It's lucky I'm a good swimmer! But it dragged me downstream...'

'Oh, Mouse, do be more careful.'

'I will, I will. I'm going back tomorrow and I'll keep my eyes open this time. I was just so excited to be there, you know.'

'I understand.'

'Would you please tell me a poem?'

'I will.
All the brownies in the den,
Say they've made friends with a hen.
But I say it's really silly,
And that they should all free Willy!'

'Lovely!'

'Let's go to sleep now mouse, shall we?'

'Let's, my dear, Topsy. Let's!'

THE MOUSE WHO LOVED HIS BICYCLE

Part III

The second day Mouse crept out of the shed as soon as the sun began to rise. He was ready to run to the witch's yard and find a way to get to the door without running into the cat. He was just passing by a flower pot when he felt his tail get caught in something. He slowly turned around, rubbing his sleepy eyes, when he heard:

'Good morning to you, little mouse!'

Mouse froze in place. Right in front of him, standing almost one foot tall, was the cat.

'You're a fast runner. First mouse to get away from me in ages. But now listen; I'm not here to harm you. Really, you can relax now. Seriously, loosen up, you look like you're going to explode.'

'What do you want from me?'

'I just want to talk to you for a moment. It kind of impressed me, how you ran away like that. What made you do it?'

'I had to get home.'

'Well, sure, but why in such a hurry?'

'Look, I can't talk about this here, Topsy will hear. Let's go under the bench, next to the front door. Be quiet until we're there, please.' Mouse said. The cat stayed quiet until they reached the bench.

'Yesterday I had to get back to Topsy. I promised her I'd get the witch to turn her into a mouse and we'll be together. She didn't

8

want me to go because she was afraid for me. But I wanted to, because I want us to be a family. So I did. Only I didn't know the witch had you. So I thought for a while I was going to die. But I couldn't let Topsy down like that. I promised her something and I'll do it and it won't be the last thing I do either, because we're going to live happily ever after too.'

'So it's love, basically, you're saying love made you do it?'

'Yes, my love for Topsy made me do it.'

'Who is this Topsy? Or, more precisely, what is she if she isn't a mouse?'

'She's a bicycle. A pink bicycle with a basket in front and ribbons on the sides.'

'You're in love with a bicycle?!'

'Yes. She's wonderful. She tells me poems and I sleep in her basket every night. When Maria takes her out, I go along and we see the world together. I want her to be able to move by herself so we can leave this place and have a life of our own.'

'How on earth did you fall in love with a bicycle?'

'We just met and fell in love. I came back to the shed really happy one day because I'd found a big piece of cheese. She was there, brand new, with her sparkling ribbons and her shiny wheels. So I thought she looked really pretty and I said it out loud. She answered with a thank you poem:

'My ribbons went from pink to red
Hearing what the mouse had said
So I thank him from the heart
And hope he'll accept this tart.'

'Did she really have a tart?'

9

'No, of course not. She's just funny like that.'

'I've never heard of a talking bike before.'

'Me neither. She's magical. She used to belong to a princess who had a palace magician and got him to make her bicycle come alive. But she was given away when the princess grew up and here she is.'

'So she loves you too?'

'Of course. More than anything. Like I love her.'

'And you defied death for her?'

'If not for her, then for whom?'

'Ok, I get it. I will help you turn Topsy into a mouse. But you must promise to teach me how to love like that.'

'What?'

'Yes, you need my help. The witch doesn't like to help anybody ever. But I can learn her spells. We'll have to make a plan. But first you have to promise me.'

'I don't think you can teach love to someone.'

'Well, you'll have to find a way. I want to have what you two have. I'm tired of being alone all the time. I want a family.'

'I could try. But how do I know you're telling the truth?'

'We'll go to the witch's house. Once you see the cages and jars filled with animals you'll see.'
'Let's go, then. The faster we do this, the better.'

THE MOUSE WHO LOVED HIS BICYCLE

With the cat by his side, getting to the witch's house was not the problem anymore. The cat allowed Mouse to ride on its back and they got there faster than you could say pickle.

'Okay, Mouse, we're going to go in through the back door. There's a kitty door so we'll have no trouble. Once we're in, we have to go into the first room on the left. That's where the witch keeps her spell book and magical ingredients. That door is always locked so I can't get in. You'll have to crawl under the door, get the key that should be dangling in the clothes hanger, to the right. Don't let the key fall in one of the jars on the floor, you'll never be able to get it out by yourself. Once you have it, bring it out, we'll unlock the door and I'll get in and read the transformation spell in the book. Then we'll take the ingredients we need and run back to your shed.'

'Cat... what's your name?'

'What? Why?'

'Since we're going to do something dangerous together, I think we should at least know each other's names.'

'Well, I don't usually tell other creatures my name. It's silly and I don't want people calling me by it.'

'Is it Strauss?'

'No.'

'Krueger?'

'No, of course not!'

ɔu stop that!'

'Oh, I know! Vikrum! It's got to be Vikrum.'

'It's Cosmo, all right? Before the witch I used to belong to a little boy who wanted to be an astronaut and he named me Cosmo.'

'Oh, wow! Nice to meet you Cosmo, my name is Twist.'

'Twist the mouse? That's really your name?'

'Yes. I know, it's funny. Twist the mouse.'

'I just realized that this makes our adventure a cosmic twist.'

'Yes... how ironic. Like it was meant to be. But look, Cat, we have to get going. I'll crawl under the door. Wait for me here.'

The little mouse did exactly as the cat told him and in a few minutes he was out with the key.

'Whew! Almost fell into a jar of jellyfish. Now lift me on your head, up to the keyhole. We're almost there!'

The mouse slowly turned the key, which was difficult with how excited he was, but just as the lock clicked and the cat pushed the door, a loud shriek sounded in the room.

'Oh! She's got a magical alarm! Quick mouse, run out! Don't stop until you get home! Hurry! Go!'

The mouse turned around and raced out of the house and as he did he could hear the loud thud of the witch's steps.

'Who dares to open my spell room?'

He couldn't hear what happened afterwards. He reached the house, climbed into Topsy's basket and pretended he had been sleeping all along. He was terrified about what could have happened to his new friend and he swore he would return to the house at night, when the witch was asleep, to check on Cosmo.

That day he told Topsy he had to go visit his cousin on the other side of town because he was too nervous to be around her. He walked around the town all day, planning his entry into the house. He was sure that the witch would have moved her spell book from the room after they triggered the alarm so he was dead worried they might never find it again. He came back home right as Topsy was about to go to sleep and asked her:

'Tell me an encouraging poem, Topsy. I'm going back to see the witch tomorrow and I need it for good luck.'

'Oh, Mouse. Here goes:
Every now and then I see a toad
Trying to get across the road
He leaps and leaps almost half across
Then comes back completely lost.
What does happen little toad,
When you're about to cross the road?
Well I realize, quite crankily
That the road travels merely horizontally
And though at times I want to cross,
I want more to just get tossed
High up in the air, so high
That I could see through space and time.'

'Topsy, you're wonderful!'

'Let's go to sleep, Mouse.'

'Okay,' Mouse whispered, sleepily.

THE MOUSE WHO LOVED HIS BICYCLE

That night a strong, cold wind blew outside and the door of the shed creaked as the tree branches hit the roof above. Mouse lay in Topsy's basket terrified.

'Oh, if it weren't for my silly dreams! I love Topsy and she loves me, we could have just as well lived together. Why did I have to start all of this? What do I do now? There's nobody to help me anymore and the witch is a dreadful creature and she probably did awful things to poor Cosmo. And I promised to teach him how to love and I can't keep that promise either. I'm such a bad friend. I can't do anything right...'

The cat reached the shed just as Mouse began talking to himself. He heard everything he had said and his feline heart melted. He had known the mouse for just one day and he'd even tried to hurt him. Yet, the little white ball of fur worried for him and felt guilty. As far as Cosmo knew, except for the little boy that used to be his master, nobody had cared about him all that much. So he felt, for the first time, like he had a real friend. He slowly pushed the door of the shed and walked in.

'Don't be blaming yourself, Twist, I'm fine.'

'Cosmo! You're alive! Are you alright? Did the witch hurt you?'

'A little bit. She knocked me around a bit with her broom, but I'm fine. She was only mad at me because I was around but she didn't figure out I was part of the plan. She thought some other witch had tried to break in. She's at war with a few of them.'

'So what did she do with the book?'

14

'She moved it in the basement and put another alarm charm around it. The entry to the basement is right under her bed but there's an air pipe that we could use without much trouble. So it's easier for us now. What we have to do is just dodge the alarm.'

'How do we do that?'

'Well, the witch's clothes have a cloaking spell on them so she never triggers the alarm herself. So what we have to do is wear her clothes. You can use a sock and I'll use a scarf.'

'A sock? Really? A sock?' Mouse asked with a tone of disgust.

'She has clean socks, Mouse!'

'Oh, alright then. So when do we leave?'

'Well, I'd say we best do it tonight cause she definitely won't expect for someone to try to steal her spell book twice in the same day.'

'Good thinking. Let's go!'

So the two friends quickly ran to the house and slowly crept inside the witch's bedroom.

'She keeps her socks in that there drawer and her scarves on that cabinet. If she wakes up, just hide. She's used to having me around so she won't think that anything's going on unless she sees you.'

The mouse did as he was told and the cat got the scarf. The witch fidgeted a little in her sleep but she didn't wake up. Cosmo and Twist then met on the roof, close to one of the air vents.

'Now look, Mouse, you have to crawl down through the vent, into the pipe, then make a right to the kitchen and push the grate

15

open from the inside. I'll be downstairs, pulling on it from the other side. I've tried to get that grate out before, it's one sturdy thing. When we take it out, I'll crawl into the pipe, to the basement where I steal the page from the book. There's no way we can take the entire book with us and it's too dark for even me to read. Now I might get stuck in the pipe because that scarf ain't exactly slippery and I ain't really small. So if I do you'll have to get me out. Let's take some butter with us, just in case.'

So they both followed the plan again and everything went perfect until...

'Mouse! I've got the page! I've got the page!'

'Great! Don't get any butter on it! Let's go!'

'I can't! What do you mean you can't?!'

'I can't feel my legs. Mouse, get over here, take the page and go! Something's happening!'

'What?!'

'I don't know, I can't see, I'm turning into something!'

The mouse quickly ran and when he got to the cat...

'Cosmo! Are you alright? I'm here. Cosmo?! Cosmo! Say something!'

The mouse tried to touch his friend but could only feel something cold and hard, like rock. Then he found the page and took it with his tiny paws.

'Cosmo... I'm scared. I found the page. Are you here? Where are you?!'

Just as he desperately tried to see something, a ray of moonlight reflected from a neighboring roof and fell through a crack next to the basement ceiling, right to where he was standing. So he saw that his friend had turned into stone. He started to cry with terrible dread, feeling lost and hopeless and guilty once again. And as his tears fell down, one of them landed on the old, worn out page and sparkled in the moonlight. Mouse saw it and suddenly realized...

'I've got the page! If I could only read it and transform him back! Oh! I can't read humaaan! What is this? It's symbols! This is the full moon, and this is... the wind blowing through the leaves and this is... I've got it! Here goes: when the wind blows under the full moon, you will rise like the lightning and transform from the womb into... a cat!'

The table started to shake under them and Cosmo's skin started to crack. From under the rock spots of fur appeared. In a moment he was shaking off the last pieces of stone and he was as alive as he'd ever been.

'I feel amazing! Mouse! You saved me!'

'Cosmo! I'm sorry Cosmo!'

'It's alright. Let's get out of here, quickly.'

'I don't need the page anymore. I know the spell.'

'Good. Let's put it back in the book, then. I don't want the witch hunting for me all her life because she figured out I stole her spell.'

'Here! Now let's go!'

So back they crawled, through the pipes, and they got to the shed with their furs all murky and covered in butter.

'Topsy! Topsy, wake up! I have the spell! I can do it now, because it's the full moon. Wake up!'
'Oh, Mouse! I'm so sleepy. But very well, do the spell... Oh, wait! Mouse... what do you want to turn me into?'

'A mouse, of course.'

'Well, I was thinking... wouldn't you rather be a different creature? Like a puppy?'

'I could be a puppy...'

'I'd love to be a puppy.'

'Puppies live longer than mice, the cat said.'

'Fine, puppies it is.'

So the next day when she walked into her shed, Maria sadly discovered her bike wasn't there anymore. But the sadness didn't last very long, because out of a box crawled two adorable white puppies and a lovable, although fairly greasy, cat. She vouched to take care of them and, as you can imagine, she most certainly did and they all lived happily ever after and Topsy made up one happy poem:

'Once there was a little white mouse
Who wanted to have a spouse.
He managed to befriend a cat
Trick a witch and wear a hat.
And one lovely summer day,
Luck happened to blow his way:
The pink bike he loved so dearly
Turned into a puppy clearly!
So he followed right along
And now they both sing this song!
And the cat that helped their chance,
Learned to love and learned to dance!'

THE PANDA THAT NEVER LOST A FRIEND

'I don't understand most things', Pandu thought to himself. 'I must not be very smart. I surely don't know why it rains. I remember my mom telling me that the world is thirsty at times. It feels like something is missing. But I don't know where to find it. Because it's missing. So there you go... that means I must not be very smart.'

'Why are you sad again, Pandu?' a blackbird asked before landing on his shoulder.

'I am worried about the caterpillar.'

'Why is that?'

'Mr. Caterpillar said he is going to die.'

'And what does that mean?'

'It means we can't be friends anymore.'

'Why is that?'

'Because he won't share my bamboo leaves anymore. Or sleep behind my ear. Or wake me up in the morning. Or sing happy birthday, to me. We won't do anything together anymore.'

'And does that mean you can't be friends?'

'I don't know. Doesn't it?'

'If someone were leaving the forest to go,' the blackbird paused, 'on a long vacation. Would you still be friends?'

'Yes!'

'Even if you were far away?'

'Even if...'

'Well, then can't you also still be friends with Mr. Caterpillar?'

'Oh... You're right, Miss Blackbird. You're right. I'm sorry. I think I must not be very bright. I didn't think of it that way. But Mr. Caterpillar won't be coming back, will he? And you see, that makes me very sad. Very, very sad. Like I already miss him, Miss Blackbird,' the panda said. His eyes filled with large tears as he stared towards the ground feeling miserable.

'My dear Pandu... what if I flew away from this forest and started a family? And what if I could never come back because I had to take care of my babies, would we still be friends?'

'Yes. But I would come and visit you and play with the little baby blackbirds.'

'But what if I was so far away that you couldn't? Or what if you had your own little baby pandas and couldn't leave them alone? Would we still be friends?'

'Yes. Yes, Miss Blackbird. You're right.' Pandu said, but tears continued to roll down his cheeks.

'Pandu, has anyone ever told you what happens when a caterpillar dies?'

'Yes. You did. It goes away on a long vacation.'

'But something else also happens, Pandu. Do you know how butterflies are born?'

'No. But they are beautiful.'

'Yes, they are. Pandu, butterflies are born out of caterpillars.'

'They are?!'

'Yes. The caterpillar goes to sleep for a long time and wakes up as a butterfly. But it's not like how you and I go to sleep. The caterpillar actually dies, but at the same time it transforms into a butterfly.'

'Because butterflies are not caterpillars. So the caterpillar has to die, otherwise the butterfly would be a caterpillar?' Pandu asked.

'Exactly!'

'So Mr. Caterpillar will become a butterfly?!'

'Do you think that will happen?'

'Yes! Or... maybe... no. No. I understand now. A butterfly will be born, but it won't still be Mr. Caterpillar. It will just be a butterfly. Will that butterfly be my friend?'

'I think there's a good chance it will be, yes.'

'So I will have two friends then?'

'Yes you will.'

'That's not so bad...'

'No, it's not.'

'Mr. Caterpillar goes on a long vacation and I also get a new friend. I like new friends. Do butterflies eat bamboo?'

'Some do.'

'Good. We'll share my bamboo leaves. And he'll sleep behind my ear. I'll take care of him until Mr. Caterpillar comes back. I'll miss him though. But I'll take care of his butterfly for him.'

'I think that's just what he would have wanted...'

THE BEAR AND THE BOOK

Part I

'Now look at it! What on earth could that be?' the bear thought.

'It's all brown, like tree bark. But solid, like a rock. It opens as though it were made of leaves, and there's all sorts of symbols all over it. It is definitely magical. If only I could understand the symbols! I have to show this to someone! Who could possibly know what it is?!' The bear just stood there and pondered this question for a moment, recalling all the animals in the forest in his mind.

'The fox! The fox should know what it is! He always visits the villages around the forest! He must have seen this before! Maybe he even knows how to decipher it!' the bear realized. He ran quickly to meet the fox, who as everyone knew, was on his afternoon break, dozing by the river, waking up every once in a while to scare the fish.

'Jonas! Jonas Fox! Wake up, Jonas Fox!'

The fox slowly proceeded to open an eye, as if out of mere pity. One of its paws was touching the clear water and no fish seemed to be in sight, though the river was usually swarming with friendly families of tiny fish.

'Yes, Bear? Why do you have to wake me during my break?'

'I found something!'

'You found something. We live in the forest Bear, we find something new every day. It's not really worth waking me up for.'

'I found something really new, Fox! Look at it!' The bear pulled out the book and fluttered its pages in front of the fox.

'Oh... one of those things. What do you want with it?'

'What is it?'

'It's a book, Bear.'

'What is a book, Fox?'

'It's something that humans look at. Sometimes they mumble when they look at it. Children do it mostly. I have no idea what the point of all of it is. It's strange too; sometimes it makes them happy, other times it makes them sad. It makes you crazy, I tell you. You should really get rid of it.'

'But I want to know what it says, Jonas!'

'Why do you care what it says? Do you want to just stare at something and then be miserable? I've seen that happen to a little girl once. The one that used to pet me before her parents saw her. She cried for two hours after looking at one of those things. She kept saying something about a love story, I can't speak human very well, so I don't know what exactly, but it seemed to make her really sad.'

'A love story... Do you think there's a love story in here?'

'I don't know, Bear. Could be anything.'

'I love love stories! Can you read it, Fox?'

'I can't, Bear. No animal can. Only humans can read. And not all of them can either.'

'Is there one that does nearby?'

'What do you want to do, Bear? Go meet a human with a book in your teeth? He'd probably shoot at you.'

'I want to see what's in here, Fox! I want to read the story!'

'What if it's not a story?'

'What else could it be?'

'I don't know... That's a good question. What else could be in here?'

'Fox, I'm going to learn to read. You listen to me! I'm going to do it!'

'Fine by me! Go learn to read! I have to go back to sleep. I have some hunting to do tonight and this conversation isn't helping me any.'

'Thank you, Fox! After I learn to read I'm going to tell you the story!'

'Great, Bear. Now go somewhere else, please.'

'Goodbye, Jonas!'

So the bear went off to think of a plan. He stopped in a clearing by the river bank and started throwing rocks into the water, waiting for an idea to jump out of it.

Strangely enough, that day he didn't have to wait long at all...

THE BEAR AND THE BOOK

As the bear stood by the river bank wondering how on earth he could learn to read, seemingly impossible obstacles came to his mind.

First of all, none of the animals he was friends with spoke human. Jonas Fox only spoke a little but he would never take the time to teach it to someone else. He thought that since he had learned it all by himself, so should others. A poor way of looking at the world, indeed.

Of the other animals, the only one known for speaking human was an old, grumpy owl who lived in a tall fir-tree. So grumpy was she, that very few animals ever exchanged pleasantries or any other form of conversation with her. In fact, nobody really knew if the owl could speak the language. What if she didn't? The rumor that she did was older than the bear himself, and in years not one shred of evidence to support the claim had ever appeared.

As luck would have it, though, as Bear was getting ready to leave the river bank and head for his favorite berry bush, a little higher on the trail, he heard a rustle of leaves and an unusual high pitched sound. A child laughing. A little girl, to be more precise, that went by the name of Krinkle.

It was Krinkle's laughter that earned her the nickname Krinkle. Perhaps not the most common nickname for a little girl, but suitable nonetheless. She had just woken up after dozing on the river bank where she had been skipping stones through the water. Her hair was up in two ponytails, but it still went down to her elbows. She was also missing one of her front teeth. Krinkle lived in the nearby village and was getting ready to enter her first year of school. She knew that part of the forest better than her own backyard, and snuck out almost every day through a hole under the fence to go to the riverside and feed the birds and fish. This kind and joyful activity made her many friends among the small creatures of the forest. Surprisingly, the grumpy old owl was among them.

When Bear heard her, he quickly hid behind a tree. He loved children, but knew the effect he had on them. Whenever they saw him, they'd yell and scurry away, climb a tree or, which Bear always found amusing, pretend to be dead. Bear actually enjoyed the ones who would play dead the most. He would sniff around them for a few minutes, pretend to smell something stinky, and would then fake a dramatic death scene, at the end of which he would fall as though lifeless next to the child. Minutes after Bear would act this out, the child would get up, not believing his luck, and run away. This started a rumor in the village that there were poisonous flowers in the forest whose smell could take out even a bear. As such, most children were forbidden to smell any type of flower they might encounter.

Fortunately, Krinkle loved flowers and did not believe in such nonsense and was busy putting together a bouquet of forest flowers. Once in a while she would stop to throw some crumbs down for the birds. As luck would have it, not even a few moments had passed when the owl made her way to a branch above Krinkle and started hooting to make her presence known.

'Feathers!' Krinkle called. 'What are you doing up there? I've got yummy brownie crumbs for you! Come taste!'

The owl flew down to a rock that gave her a perfect pecking angle for the crumbs. She had a soft look in her eyes and it was obvious that she cared for the child. Krinkle sat next to her, gave her a hug and started gently patting her brown wings.

'I missed you, Feathers! I couldn't come see you yesterday because mommy took me to see Aunt Mary's ponies. Three ponies she has, and a big ol' shepherd dog. I think she likes big animals. But I like small animals. Like you, Feathers! Tell me a story, Feathers! I want to hear a story! Tell me a story!'

The owl looked curiously at her as though she understood but had no idea what she was talking about. She turned her eyes to see if there were any other animals in sight, and even flew away briefly to scout the area from above. Luckily, Bear was right under a big tree branch so she didn't notice him at all. Then, she came back , turned her head one more time, took a deep breath and said in a low, rough voice.

'What story, would you like to hear today, Krinkle?'

'I want to hear a story about... about... about a princess and an owl and a pony. I lost my book, Feathers! I lost my book with the princess story. Tell me the princess story, Feathers!'

'Very well, Krinkle. But you should go looking for your book. It is a priceless thing to have.'

'I will, Feathers. Right after you tell me the story.'

The bear by now was both shocked and amazed. He couldn't believe how good the forest had been to him that day. Not only did he find a book, but it was a book about a princess, and someone knew how to read it! And not just someone, but one of the animals in the forest. His jaw dropped in amazement and he barely took a breath. All he wanted was to hear the story unfold.

Part III

'Once upon a time, in a castle far-far away, there lived a beautiful princess. So beautiful was she that when she was born...' No sooner had Feathers started the story than a voice was heard.

'Krinkle! Krinkle! I know you're here somewhere, Krinkle!' a woman called. 'There you are!' She pushed some leaves aside with her hand and appeared from behind an oak. 'I searched the entire river bank for you!'

'I'm sorry, mommy!' said Krinkle and ran into her mother's arms. 'Feathers was telling me a story!'

'Oh, Krinkle! You and your talking owl again. Come on home. I made tootsie rolls!'

'Tootsie rooooooolls!' Krinkle squeaked and started jumping up and down, with a wide smile and her missing tooth showing.

'Let's gooo!' she said and started pulling her mother's hand.

'Byeeee, Feeeeatheeeers!' was the last thing she said before she disappeared behind the oak.

'Oh... My... How she always leaves me like that,' the owl sighed.

'Miss Owl?'

'Pardon me? Who said that?!'

'Don't fly away, Miss Owl, I only mean really, really well!'

'Bear?! Is that you? Come out from behind that tree, please, I can see one of your feet.'

'Here I am!'

'Well... Good. So what? You heard me talk to the little girl, right? Big deal! Just don't tell anyone! It isn't anyone's business!'

'Miss Owl! Miss Owl! Miss Owl! You can speak human! That is the most wonderful-est thing in the world!'

'Bear, please, don't bore me to death using poor grammar. Tell me what... Do you want to keep quiet about this?'

'I want to reeead!'

'I beg your pardon?'

'I want to read, Miss Owl. I want you to teach me how to read, and if you do I won't be saying nothing to no one!'

'Please, Bear, in all the years I've been in this forest, never have I heard something so silly. How could YOU possibly learn to read?'

'Just like you did!'

'Preposterous! I'm an owl, Bear!'

'So?'

'I... Well I can't teach you!'

'Why?'

'I can't!'

31

'Why?'
'You wouldn't learn!'

'Yes, I would! Please, oh please, I want to learn to read the princess love story if it's the last thing I do!'

'I can't teach you, Bear!'

'Yes you can!'

'No! I won't!'

'You're just being mean!'

'So what if I am?! I can be any way I want!' the owl said and started flapping her wings.

'Oh no!' The bear realized that this might be his only chance to ever learn the story so, impolite as it was, he said:

'Either you tell me, or I tell everyone you can speak human and every animal in this forest will come looking for you to learn how to speak human themselves. Now... I may be wrong, but I think some of them won't ask nicely, like I just did.'

The owl froze in mid-air, then slowly descended towards the ground.

'Bear, you silly animal. I can't teach you to read.'

'Then I'll tell!'

'No, Bear. I really can't.' she said in a low voice. 'I don't know how to read.' The owl continued, obviously ashamed of her own statement.

'Oh...' The bear paused and pondered for a moment, while the owl remained motionless, her head hanging down.

'Why... don't you learn then?'

'Excuse me?!' asked the owl, awestruck.

'Yes! We'll learn how to read together!'

'Lovely plan, Bear, but how?!'

'Your little girl can teach us!'

'Krinkle?!'

'Yes, her, whatever her name is.'

'Krinkle can't read Bear. That's why I tell her the story. She just looks at the pictures.'

'So how do you know the story, then?'

'I made it up...This autumn she'll go to school and learn to read and see that I'm nothing but a dumb animal.'

'Don't say that, Miss Owl. You can speak human! That's wonderful!'

I used to belong to someone, Bear. I wasn't born in the forest. That's how I learned human. I could speak it before I could even properly speak our tongue. It just happened, it's not something I did.

'Yes it is, Miss Owl. Mitsy the cat doesn't speak human. Or Rufus the pooch. You're the only animal I ever heard of that does. You're magical, Miss Owl!'

'Please, Bear!' said the owl, blushing.

'If Krinkle learns to read, do you think she'd teach us?'
'She would, yes. She's a lovely child. Much better than my owners used to have.'

'So let's ask her, Miss Owl! Pleeeease!'

'Very well, Bear. I will ask her and we will learn to read. But please promise me you won't tell anyone!'

'I swear on my honey that I won't, Miss Owl.'

'Good, Bear. Now can I go to my nest and rest, please?'

'Yes, Miss Owl! Have a wonderful time nesting!'

'Bye, Bear!' the owl said flapping her wings. As she flew away a warm smile spread across her beak. She realized that the best moments of her life were perhaps yet to come.

THE BEAR AND THE BOOK

Part IV

'Be quiet, Bear! She'll hear us!'

'Miss Owl, one of your claws is poking my nose. Please be still.'

'I can't see her.'

'Of course you can't see her, you're a night bird. I can see her just fine.'

'So what do you want me to do?! She always sleeps at night.'

'I want you to tell her! Tell her to teach us to read.'

'I can't Bear. We've been over this. Now shush so I can hear her!'

Now you may have already guessed what happened. Feathers never told Krinkle she couldn't read. The shame of the little girl finding out was too much for her to bear. Instead, she had taken to Bear's idea and decided to learn. Her plan, in fact, was to learn before Krinkle could, and let the truth remain hidden forever. So when Krinkle started attending school, Bear and Feathers would hide below a window in her house every afternoon to spy on her homework and learn everything at the same time as she was. What they wanted most was to learn the alphabet. Bear would take a good look at what Krinkle was drawing on her notebooks every day, and then copy the symbols into the ground using a stick. They found a hidden clearing in the forest where they could do this undisturbed.

Sometimes the work was overwhelming. They had to bring water so that the ground was moist and fit for writing in every day. Then they had to wait for the ground to dry. It was already autumn so several rains had fallen and threatened to erase all their work. To save it they stood in the rain for hours, holding umbrellas made of leaves over the letters. They'd both caught a cold and then nursed each other back to health with tea and forest medicine.

In all truth, it was the first time for either of them to be working on something so hard or so closely with someone else. As far as they remembered, they hadn't really struggled for much. The forest kept them safe, well fed and simple. They hadn't known worry, haste, or the fear of losing something great before.

Within a few months of working steadily every day, they became very different animals than when they started. Then... one day...

'Miss Owl! Miss Owl! Come down! I got it! I finally got it!'

'It's morning bear, I'm tired and I just went to sleep. What do you want?'

'I found out the last one. Today is the last one!' the bear said with, quite possibly, the most enthusiasm ever seen in a bear. He jumped up and down frantically while hugging himself. The realization of what the bear was talking about slowly dawned on the owl. When the fact appeared clearly before her, she jumped to her feet, out of the tree, and as she was heading towards the ground she felt a tremendous wave of joy passing through each and every one of her feathers.

'Are you sure, Bear? It is the last one?!'

'The last one, Miss Owl! I want us to go write it down now before I forget it.'

'Let's go, Bear!' And off they scurried towards the clearing, feeling like all the months of hard work and learning had been worth it. Finally, after all the years spent not knowing what made humans laugh or cry, what made them shine and talk and leave their homes, they would finally understand. They would finally know why humans were not just happy with living in the forest and had to go off and build cities. Huge things that looked and hummed like giant bees but were missing the wings, and were multi-colored.

They reached the clearing. Bear quickly grabbed a stick and drew a shape on the ground. It looked like a mountain tilted to the ground.

'They call it "zee", Miss Owl, and it's used in words like zebra and crazee.'

'Zee... what a strange sound. Sounds a bit like a bee but like a really high-pitched bee, like a bee kicked in the shins.'

'Yes, it does! I thought of just about the same thing. Now, Miss Owl. Do you know what I've got here, behind my back?'

'Yes, I do, Bear.'

'What? How?'

'You're not holding it straight and it's showing.'

'Oh, pardon me.'

'Now... do you know what I'm holding here behind my back?'

'Yes I do, Bear, I've already seen it!'

'Oh... well. Good enough. Here it is!' the bear said gloriously and pulled out the book. 'Let's reeeaaaad it!'

They looked at it as if it were a sacred object. They laid it on a large flat boulder, in the middle of the clearing. The bear slowly opened the cover of the book and turned the first, white page.

'Mas... Mas... Mas... what is that, Miss Owl?'
'A T, Bear.'

'Mast... er... ing... t... t... t... Mast... er... ing t...'

'The, Bear, the.'

'Mast... er... ing... THE... arrr... arrr... arrrt... o o o o offf frrrrren...ch.'

'Oh, my Lord, vive la France!'

'C... c... c-o-o...'

'Coo, Bear, coo.'

'Coo...king.'

'Mast-er-ing the arrr-t of frr-en-ch coo-king.'

'Bear, I think you got that last word wrong.'

'No, Miss Owl, look there on the ground, that's a g all the way, and that's a K and an I.'

'Bear... do you know what cooking is?'

'No, Miss Owl! What is it?! Is it a princess? Is it a castle?! Is it a pony?'

'No, Bear. It's... something completely different.'

'You seem sad, Miss Owl. What is it?'

'Nothing, Bear, it's just that... this is not a story book.'

'Yes it is! What else are books for?'

'Well, it's not. It's a... cooking book. Cooking is when humans make food for themselves.'

'Oh... so no story?!'

'Actually... I'm afraid not. No story, Bear. I'm sorry. I'm very, very sorry.'

'It's ok, Miss Owl. You didn't know. At least now Krinkle will understand why you didn't read her the story.'

'I can't believe that all this time that child was looking at pictures of food.'

'Food is good, Miss Owl. Krinkle is a good girl. She taught us how to read.'

'Yes, Bear, she did. And so did you. Without you I would have never found out that this is a cook book.'

'What do we do now, Miss Owl?'

'Well, Bear. I don't know.'

'I want to read a story, Miss Owl.'

'So do I, Bear.'

'Why don't we write a story that we can read together, Miss Owl?'

'What do you mean, Bear?!'

'Well, you know a story. You know a story that you told to Krinkle. Why don't you write it?'

39

'Well, I... never thought about that. I suppose I could. You know, Bear, you're pretty smart for an animal with bad grammar.'
'Thank you, Miss Owl.'

'You want to start writing the story now?'

'Why not? I have my stick!'

'Good. Let's get to it, then.'

'Once upon a time, in a castle far-far away, there lived a beautiful princess. So beautiful she was that when she was born...'

THE BUBBLE BOY AND HIS FLYING MACHINE

Once upon a time, in a small town perched on each of three small hills overlooking a river valley, there lived Doodle... also called the Bubble Boy. The townsfolk had given him this name because he had the extraordinary ability to make giant bubbles of soap in his tiny laboratory at the top of Reinmar hill. Once he made a bubble so large, it was bigger than his entire home. It swelled up and pushed out through the open windows and the chimney, causing the house to look like a sweater covering a child who had outgrown it.

Doodle dreamed of one day flying off to the moon in one of his bubbles. He knew it was impossible because the bubbles blew up when they reached a certain height, but he still hoped that o he would figure out a way to make it happen. Until one sunny day in August, an old, gray man walked through the door.

'Are you Doodle, the Bubble Boy?'

'Yes,' Doodle said while pouring a jar of blue soap pellets into a small tub. 'What can I help you with? I do birthdays, but I don't like the circus, and they told me my bubbles aren't sturdy enough to be in the movies.'

'No, that's not what I have come to talk to you about. See, I am an inventor. And I want to build a flying machine that stays in the air using... bubbles.'

'Wow! I'd love to do that! But my bubbles always blow up after a while. I'm afraid the machine would crash mighty fast.'

'But what if we found a way to keep the bubble from bursting?' the inventor asked.

'You could. But you'd have to keep adding soap and water all the time!'

'Well, there's plenty of water in the clouds, isn't there? And we could just take soap with us, as fuel. Every vessel runs on some form of fuel.'

'But Mister, even if you did have soap and water all the time, what about the wind and cloud and storms? Soap bubbles aren't cut out for that!'

'Aren't they? Have you ever flown in a balloon, Doodle?'

'Once, when I was little. My mum and dad took me. It was really great! That's when I decided I wanted my own balloon. But then I realized that if I make soap bubbles instead, I can have as many balloons as I want!'

'You're right there. Soap bubbles fly when they're filled with hot air. Just like...?'

'Hot air balloons.'

'Precisely. Now, I made some calculations and it seems to me that if you managed to make a bubble with walls thick and flexible enough, it would handle storms much better than regular balloons. A soap bubble can change its shape so easily that you can't tear it. You can only pop it. But if you add enough soap and water, any hole would be covered instantly. It just patches itself up.'

'That's a good point, Mister. But if you know all that, what do you need me for?'

'Well, Doodle, I can make the machine that blows the bubbles and holds the passengers and has tanks for water and soap. But I can't tell what ingredients I need for the bubbles, or how to mix them.'

'Oh, I can do that. That's all I do all day long.'

'Perfect! So we have a deal, then? We'll build a flying machine together?'

'Yes! Yes we do! You know Mister... I've been waiting for someone to ask me that all my life!'

Doodle and the inventor began work on their plan immediately. Soon enough, the laboratory was filled with sketches and blueprints of flying machines. Doodle had quickly found the recipe for the perfect bubble; after all, he had been working on it all his life. The challenge, however, was to keep the bubble connected to the machine. A hot air balloon has strings tying it to the basket. But how were they supposed to tie-up a ball of liquid?

Doodle thought and thought, but he could not come up with a solution. The inventor seemed oblivious to this issue. He worked on designing the perfect lightweight tanks and a pressurized capsule to keep them safe and warm, instead of a traditional basket.

One early morning Doodle was sitting on the steps of his laboratory, stroking his pet sloth. He'd found Hewey on his doorstep when he was only a pup and he took him in and cared for him. Because everyone thought Doodle was a bit off his noodle, Hewey was his only true friend.

'What do I do, boy? I know that this problem has a solution, I can feel it inside me. I just can't get it out of me so I don't know what it is yet. I can't connect the dots.'

Hewey didn't take Doodle's grave concern to heart. He was more preoccupied with trying to move his bed from the shade into the sunlight so he could take a warm and comfortable nap. At first he grabbed the crate, for his bed was merely a wooden crate, by one of its leather belts and started pulling as hard as he could. But the crate would not budge an inch. He stopped for a moment and looked at it confused. He stretched out with his paws spread and his belly on the ground, as if ready to give up. Then, all of a sudden, he jumped back on his feet. He smelled the crate, looked at it and something like a grin appeared on his face. He then proceeded to move to the other side of the crate and push it in his desired direction. He strained for a bit but eventually the box moved and he happily jumped in and almost instantly fell asleep.

Why am I telling you this you may wonder? Well, because in watching the sloth's efforts, our Doodle had an epiphany.

'That's iiiit! That's iiiiit! Mister! Mister!' He ran
into the lab and woke up the old man who had fallen asleep at his desk.

'What?! What?! What's the matter, boy?!'

'I got it, I got it!'

'You got what, what?'

'We're not going to pull the capsule! We're going to push it! We're going to have ourselves an upside down flying balloon! We're going to be sitting on top of the bubble!'

'Doodle... that's brilliant! How did I not think about that one myself! You are a genius, boy!'

'You know sir... if we're to be honest, I'm really no smarter than a sloth.'

The scientist look puzzled and Doodle didn't explain any further. He just walked out and happily stretched out, next to Hewey, in the sunlight.

Doodle and the inventor worked day and night on the flying machine, and by the end of the summer it was almost done. They only had a few more days to go and they were working restlessly to get every detail in place. The two soap reservoirs on the side of the capsule were connected to two thin hoses than ran underneath it and poured the soap inside a round plastic jar. Above it, there was a propeller, and underneath it a funnel so the entire mechanism looked a bit like an hourglass with a propeller on top. Another small hose ran into the jar, mixing in just the right quantity of water for the existing soap. The mixture then ran down into the funnel and as the propeller turned faster and faster, a bigger and bigger bubble appeared below.

Now the problem was figuring out how to get the capsule to sit still on top of the bubble. They were already experimenting with a gyroscope and the contraption got steadier by the hour.

However, something still troubled Doodle. He couldn't tell exactly what it was but he had trouble falling asleep at night. He felt like he'd forgotten something that he couldn't leave behind. There was plenty of room for him and the doctor in the capsule, they were already stocking up on supplies and the building of the flying machine was going according to plan. If the weather was good enough for a launch, they would set sail for the first time that very week-end. So what didn't fit?

One night, he had a particularly difficult time falling asleep so he woke up the next morning tired and surly. He went into the kitchen, fixed himself a cup of tea and sat at the table with his head resting on his hands. His eyes were closing and he was just about to fall asleep again.

At this precise moment, Hewey entered the kitchen. He looked at his master with a puzzled expression. He climbed on one of the chairs and bent over the table to smell the tea and the lumps of sugar. He was delighted by the sweet smell of tea in the morning. Feeling a bit sorry for his master, who did not seem to enjoy the scenery as much, he decided to wake him up.

So he slowly crept behind Doodle and started clambering on the back of his chair. Doodle must have been really tired, because at first he didn't feel a thing. When Hewey crawled from the chair on top of his shoulders and started petting his head gently, he suddenly opened his eyes and for a moment felt like screaming at the top of his lungs. Luckily enough, he recognized in a split second that it was only Hewey sitting on his shoulders and gently patting his bushy hair.

At that moment, Doodle almost burst to tears. For he suddenly realized what he was leaving behind: his one and only friend, Hewey. He gently grasped the sloth and set him down, then they both went to have a morning nap in Doodle's bed.

That day Doodle convinced the inventor that they hadn't been thinking properly about the capsule all along. It wasn't supposed to be built for two, but for three. His sloth was going with him. Luckily enough, the professor understood and agreed to please the boy. So they started again, rebuilding everything from scratch. Now, of course they weren't ready to sail at the end of the summer anymore. They had to wait for autumn and winter to pass so they could leave in good weather. But they did, without a sigh or a quarrel and when the bubble rose from the ground, in the clear, crisp air of spring, there were three best friends traveling on it. And this is where our story ends.

THE MAGICAL HOUSE OF DOORS

Part I

Jean first saw the house through the train's window, when she was on her way to visit her grandparents. It looked just like a regular house, except the walls were made of many different doors, all standing next to one another. One was blue, dressed with white time-worn curtains, another was tall, brown and looked sturdy, though the wood had chipped here and there. She decided to ride her bike back and examine the place a little closer. With the open field in front of it and chickens pecking their way all around it, the house looked as if pulled out of a story and planted there.

She only made it back the next afternoon, and almost fell off her bike right in front of the yard. The chickens were all gathered up in the coop, which was peculiar for a warm afternoon. Jean looked around to see what might have scared them, and saw a giant, dark rain cloud drawing near.

'Great... got here just in time to leave. Gosh, that thing is moving fast. I'll never make it home on time.' Just then, the sky lit up followed by a roar of thunder. 'Well, I'm not going anywhere until that cloud passes... So I guess there's only one thing I can do.'

She slowly pushed open the gate and stepped inside the yard. There was a peaceful air around the house. On top of the chicken coop, a white cat was sleeping on its belly. Behind it, a woodpecker chipped away at an old peach tree. The peaches looked like they'd just started to turn gold. The wind seemed to have stopped.

'Hello? Anybody here? Hello? I figured I wouldn't get an answer. Now which of these doors should I knock on? The blue one looks good. Here goes!'

'Yes! Who's there?!'

'Hello! My name is Jean, I was just riding my bike and I got caught in the storm. Could you please open the door?'

'Poor girl! Certainly!'

The door slowly creaked open and Jean was more than surprised to meet the kind stranger.

'Hello, I am Miss Dolly. Please, come in! Have a seat, I was just making tea. Have you ever had wheat tea?'

'No, I haven't.'

'Well, you'll love it. I don't get many visitors around here. My door isn't quite the most popular. Frisco the bear sees at least three time as many people as I do.'

49

The old lady went about her tiny cottage, bringing cups and napkins and several jars of jam to the table. She even had whole wheat crackers. Everything might have appeared normal... if not for the fact that she was a mouse. Her fur was auburn and she walked on her hind legs and had a kerchief on her head, complete with ear holes. But what was Jean to do? She couldn't have just asked 'Miss, are you aware that you are a mouse?' So she just went along with it.

'So where does Frisco the Bear live, Miss Dolly?'

'Oh, just in the house, like I mentioned. You can find him behind the big, black door.'

'But the big black door's one of the walls of your house.'

'No, honey, it isn't. Look around. I have real walls.'

And indeed she did. And Jean realized she had just discovered something extraordinary.

Part II

'Does Frisco the bear have another room in this house, Miss Dolly?'

'Of course not, he owns the entire house, just like I do.'

Jean was very happy to have her suspicion confirmed.

'And does anyone else own the house, Miss?'

'Yes, there are as many of us as there are doors. Helmut the bald eagle lives behind the gray, run-down door. Oh, how foul his house smells. He likes scaring me to death too, keeps saying he's going to eat me. I swear, if he even so much tries to swallow in my direction I will go ninja on his beak!'

'I'm sure you'll be fine, Miss. This tea is just wonderful. I've never had wheat tea before. It's sweet.'

'Thank you dear!'

'And who else, except Helmut?'

'Well, there's also Helga, the platypus. Lovely creature she is. She gave me the milk I put in your tea.'

'Oh! Where else do you get milk from around here? It's pretty far from any other farm.'

'Well, from her. She just laid a few eggs and she's got extra milk.'

'Oh, dear me!'
'Are you alright, dear?'

51

'Um... Miss Dolly, I just realized, I left my bike in front of the yard. Can I please go bring it on the porch?'

'Sure, dear.'

As Miss Dolly closed the door behind her, she started coughing. Platypus milk! It took a few good minutes for her to catch her breath and, when she realized Miss Dolly hadn't checked on her, she figured she might as well try some of the other doors.

One of them was shiny and purple, and looked like it had just been waxed. With the others appearing rather dull, she took her chance on this one.

'Hello?' she said as she knocked. 'Is anyone there?'

'Why certainly!' The door's patron flamboyantly remarked as he swung the door open. 'And who might you be, young lady?'

'Hello, I am Jean. And... if you'll pardon me, what are you, more precisely?'

'I am a gentleMAN! I like to bedazzle and bewitch and my hobby is to pitch!'

'Wow, you are so full of... life. Could you please tell me what type of animal you are, though. I don't mean to be rude, I'm just curious. I want to learn.'

'I am a purple martin. Please, call me Purple Martin!'

'Is that your name or your species?'

'It's both, honey bunch!'

'I see. I have to be going now though.'

'Why, where you going?'

'I'm just going to... bike home.'

'With the storm that's coming? Girl, you must be some sort of oddball. You're staying right here. Ain't nobody leaving in the rain, not from my house. Come in! I'll fix you up some cereal and tell you my amazing life story! I've been waiting for someone to hear it for ages!'

'Why didn't you tell it to the other animals?'

'Oh, they don't talk to me. 'I guess they can't handle gentlemen. Probably used to more simple folk.'

'But I was just at Miss Dolly's and she seemed perfectly polite.'

'Well, one time, she told me that if I ever address her again, she'll go ninja on my feathers.'

'Did you say something bad to her?'

'No. I just mentioned she's a fine piece of rodent!'

'You did not say that!'

'What's wrong with that?! It's a compliment!'

'And you pretend to be a gentleman!'

'I do not pretend! I am the more gentle of all the men within a mile!'

'There are no other houses for a mile!'

'Fine, be a smarty pants! If you don't want to listen to the story, then don't! I'm used to it!'

'Oh... I didn't mean it like that. I'm sorry. Does your story say anything about this house?'

'Sure, I was one of the animals that built this house.'

'Really?'

'No kiddin'. Now sit yourself down and have a cracker. I'm going to tell you all about it!'

THE MAGICAL HOUSE OF DOORS

'Once upon a time, all the animals in the forest decided they wanted a house of their own. Not just a burrow where the water crawls in from everywhere when it rains. But a house; a real house with a roof and a door and windows, like people have. We thought we could build a village of our own, maybe right inside the forest and we would be safe and warm. But you can't just start and do something like that in the forest. Not without the blessing of the Forest Godmother.

So one day me, Frisco the bear, Viggo the wolf, Eloise the deer and a few other animals, decided to go and ask the Godmother's permission. We arrived at the sacred clearing on a full moon night and called for her. The wind started to blow and the leaves of the trees rustled, and we could hear her voice. She asked us why we came to see her. None of the animals dared make a sound.

After what seemed like forever, Frisco finally said:

'We want a house, Godmother. We want all of us to live in a house with a roof. Each animal to have the ability to keep the door of his house open or closed to whomever he pleases, and to stay out of the rain and snow anytime he wants to.'

'And why have you come to me?'

'For permission, Godmother.'

'Animals are not supposed to live in houses. The forest is your house. It is your home. The trees and the leaves are your roof. They feed you, keep you safe, dry and warm. Why do you want to be like the humans that hunt you?'

'Well... Godmother... why wouldn't we be? They don't hunt us because they live in houses. Animals hunt other animals as well.'

'You are right, Frisco, but it is not the law of things for animals to be like humans. So I must forbid it from spreading in the forest. Those of you who have come here, you will have your house. But outside and far from the forest it will be. And you will live in it, as you please. Go home now. You will wake up in your house tomorrow.'

So the next morning we woke up and we were here. Ta-da!'

'And were you happy?'

'No, not really, to tell you the truth. You don't have any privacy with this open field in front of you. We're warm now, but that's about all we are. We miss our friends. I think we're all lonely here.'

'Then why don't you go back?'

'We can't. We tried. Whenever we try to get close to a forest it keeps moving further away. We have to live like this.'

'Wow! That's kind of sad. Did you ever think about asking the Forest Godmother for permission to go back?'

'Yes, we did. But Frisco doesn't want to. He's been mad at us all these years. Says we got what we deserved and we should live with it. I think he's just really, really ashamed. He didn't want a house so badly, he did it for us mostly.'

'Is he a friendly bear?'

'He used to be very friendly. He used to love kids. He was a circus bear when he was a pup so he's really good with humans.'

'I'll go talk to him then. See if we can get this sorted out.'

'Well, to tell you the truth, I don't think that will help. But it can't hurt to try. You know his door, right?'

'Yes, the big wooden one.'

'Come back and tell me what happened.'

'I will. Bye, Mr. Blue Martin!'

'Bye, honey bunch!'

'Ugh!' Jean said under her breath and closed the door behind her.

Part IV

'Please leave! Stop pestering me! You've been here every day for two weeks now. Can't you take a hint?! I'm not going anywhere!'

'But Mister Bear, you have to. I spoke to all the other animals. They're waiting on you and they're counting on you. You can't just stay here in this house forever!'

'Why not? This is what they wanted, isn't it? To have a house. Well, they have a house now! They weren't happy before, they're not happy now either. What if we go back to the forest and they make everybody else unhappy?! Maybe they should be here. Everyone's safer that way!'

'So that's what you're worried about! You don't want to see anymore animals suffering!'

'What do you know? You're just a little girl. We've been here for years and years. I don't know how long it's been, I stopped counting. Don't you think I want to go home?'

'I... I suppose you do. But isn't there something we could do to let everybody win? If you can't go back to the forest, maybe we could plant a new forest.'

'Goedefrillops! Plant a forest!'

'Why not? A forest is just trees. I could bring you seeds and we could plant new trees. What's wrong with that?'

'It would take forever for the trees to grow. Some of the trees in the forest were over a hundred years old. And a forest is more than the sum of its trees!'

'A forest is more than the sum of its trees... That's a lovely thing to say. And I'm sure it's true. But this one would be too. Each animal that lives in this house would bring something to the spirit of the forest. You're all wonderful creatures. I don't see why your forest wouldn't be as beautiful as any other.'

'I don't know. Please go now. I want to rest. I will think about what you've said to me.'

Jean looked through the window, at the sky outside. It was clear blue and the field was green. She slowly crept out and rode her bike home. Why was he so stubborn she wondered? Why not plant a forest? What was stopping them? Should she do it by herself? Or was she supposed to let the animals just figure it out for themselves? She wanted to do good but what if they never learned that you have to fight for what you want?

'Maybe they'll learn from example,' she thought. So on that dirt road, trailing across the rail line, she decided she was going to plant a forest. 'And then we'll see...' she said to herself. 'Then we'll see.'

She came back that evening with a small hand spade. She dug seven small holes around the yard and planted seeds in each of them. Oak, beech, birch, walnut, the trees that her grandparents had around their house. She came again the next evening and the evening after that. And, by the end of the summer, there were nearly five hundred holes in the ground and some of the seeds had started sprouting.

The first day of September, when she had to return to the city, she made one last visit to the house of doors. She said goodbye to Miss Dolly, Blue Martin, Helga, even Frisco, and she tried very hard to keep herself from crying. They walked her to the train station and hid behind some bushes when her grandparents came to bring her luggage. She got on the train and waved goodbye again and felt like she would remember this summer forever.

That year, her grandparents moved to a new neighborhood. So the next summer she didn't go to the village anymore, or to the house of doors. The years passed and she thought about her forest once in a while, but remembered everything like in a dream. How could it be true? She wondered. A magical house filled with talking animals...

Then, one day, she found herself walking towards the train station. Why not see what had happened? Why try to forget about something so wonderful? She got on the same train and travelled to the village where she grew up. And surely enough, she didn't see a house made of doors on the way. Of course she didn't. She couldn't. How could anyone see anything through all those trees?

MAGICAL JOURNEYS AND ADVENTURES

CLIMBING THE MAGIC MOUNTAIN

Part I

I met the little girl who lived in the magical forest one day early in the morning as I was walking to the river to get water. At the time I was living in a small village, at the foothill of a tall mountain.

It was so tall, that if you climbed it, after you went above the clouds, in the distance you could see yet another layer of clouds, as far away and as thick as the first one. It was a simple chance encounters like many of you may have had in your lives. I sat down next to the clear stream, without any rush or concern. I leaned my clay pot towards the water and as the brim was ready to be touched by the first drop, I noticed a golden reflection in the water's ripples. I stopped, enchanted for a moment, as it looked as though a golden ray had fallen from the sun into the water. As my mind pondered the beauty of that bright, golden triangle, the world seemed to have stopped. And then, as if out of nowhere, I heard a voice as soft and joyful as a parade of butterflies.

'What are you doing here?' the voice asked, and for a short while I thought I'd imagined it, it was so delicate. 'Are you thirsty? Is your pot thirsty?'

I turned around, smiling at the idea of my pot being thirsty, and there she was. She barely passed my knee in height, and was wearing a dress made out of what seemed to be tree leaves. Her hair shone so bright you could barely look her way, and her eyes were as green as the leaves of the old forest. You can imagine that I immediately assumed she was a forest fairy. They helped children who get lost in the woods find their way home. On the way, they would teach them to speak to an animal of the forest. Afterwards, that animal would follow the child for the rest of his life and defend him at any cost. I imagined however that I was neither a child nor was I lost. But as soon as the thought came to my mind something like a tiny door opened in the back of my head and I knew that neither of those two assumptions were true.

'I have to take you home,' she said. 'I have to take you to where you belong. I'll keep you safe along the way, but you have to believe it to be true. As long as you believe that you are safe, you will be.'

The irony of the situation amused me. A little girl a foot high promised to protect me on my way home, which was a mere quarter of an hour away.

'Come with me. You'll have to walk a little slower as you're taller than me, but we will get there. If you believe that we will get there, we will get there.'

I did believe I was going to get home, I just didn't understand how this miraculous creature had stumbled onto me out of all people. Of all the lost children in the world, was I really the one who needed help the most?

CLIMBING THE MAGIC MOUNTAIN

Part II

'Come! Follow me!' the little girl said.

'My home is the other way. There, to the east.'

'No. That is not your home. That is your house. We are going home now. Follow me' she said again and started walking with small, fast steps. It was as if she was treading on an invisible layer of snow that covered the ground. She was barefoot but the soles of her feet were clean and the leaves on her dress were alive as though they'd never been taken off their tree. I started to follow her in silence.

We walked for a few hours, deeper and deeper into the forest where I'd never been before. The trees seemed to be changing color. The further we went, the more the green of the leaves seemed to reflect a golden light. At times it was dense that it appeared you could cut through the golden rays. There was more and more light around us as we advanced and it seemed to be coming from all directions.

'Where are we?'

'We are where birds learn to sing.' And no sooner had she spoken than we came across a flood of light. We'd just stepped into what seemed to be a magical clearing. I looked around and up and down, not believing my eyes. The old tall oaks standing around were filled with birds. Every branch appeared to have a different kind of bird perched on it. They were all looking towards the center of the clearing. They seemed to have not noticed or care about my presence.

'Look!' the little girl said, pointing to the same place on the ground. A wisp of golden smoke seemed to be coming out of the earth. It rose a few feet, then seven birds flew towards it in a circle, grabbing it by the edges with their beaks and tore it into

67

seven thin golden threads. Each then swirled in the air, wrapped the thread around itself and, in perfect synchronicity with the others, opened its wings wide, almost violently.

For a moment they seemed to be frozen in mid-air. I felt my heart pounding as they started falling towards the ground, only to reverse in flight at the last moment and swoop back to their initial branches.

'They have all learned to sing now. All seven of them.'

'How? How did that teach them to sing?'

'They found their song. Their song rose from the ground and they took it. It's the same song for all of them, they only sing it in different voices. This is why I brought you here. It is the same song for you and me as well. You just have to hear through the voice and realize you're singing.'

'I am singing?'

'Yes, you are singing all the time. All the time! You just can't hear your singing as it is. You can't hear it like you've just seen it. That is how the song sounds.'

'The song we all sing sounds like it looks like?'

'Yes. That is not strange at all. You will understand as we get closer to home. There is nothing more simple than the song. That's why it is beautiful and why it hides.'

'The song is hiding?'

'We are hiding it with all we do. It is why you cannot hear it anymore. You do sometimes. You hear it in your dreams from time to time or when you are awake and you encounter something that makes the world stop. You heard it today when we met. You just have to remember. But we must go now. I showed you the song so you could hear it. Now you have to touch it so you can sing it.'

'Am I not singing it already?'

'You are. Somewhere. You have to sing it louder. You have to sing it so you can hear it. So we're going where you can touch it.'

'That sounds... Wonderful.'

I looked at this magical, alive piece of the world with amazement and admiration. She seemed to be powered by something outside my world and you could see through her, like through water. There was nothing but good inside and it sparkled like a river in clear sunlight.

If this was a dream I did not know what I had done to deserve it. I followed her out of the clearing through a gap in a hedge and arrived at nothing but the widest field I could imagine. There were only red poppies, tall grass and berry bushes as far as my eyes could see. A narrow trail started right at our feet.

'Come! We have to meet Puddle,' she said and walked away again. I could do nothing but follow her.

CLIMBING THE MAGIC MOUNTAIN

For what seemed to be hours and hours we walked and I wondered where the evening had gone. The sun set at the far edge of the field with a masterful display of every shade of rose nature had probably ever created. The trail and the scenery seemed to be never-ending. On and on we walked until the soles of my feet started to hurt unbearably. I asked to stop but the little girl wouldn't answer. Her feet were still clean and her dress of leaves was well alive, but different. It was no longer made out of oak leaves, but smooth blades of fine grass.

'Please stop. Please, please, please, I can't go any further!'

'We have to go. We are going to meet Puddle. Puddle will help us get you home. He's not far off now.'

'I can see nothing ahead or behind except this endless field! I don't know where I am, what world I am in. I don't know how I am ever going to get home from here!' I said and turned around to look at the trail. Only there wasn't one. Any trace of it had disappeared from behind us.

'If you believe that we will get there we will get there. Belief is not something you say or assume. It is something you do. You have to believe and if you believe you will walk and if you walk you will believe.'

'I am not magical like you are! I am a normal person! My feet are sore, dirty and tired. I just want to rest. I need to rest.'

'There is no time for rest. We have to go meet Puddle. It is not far now.'

'How much longer is it?'

'As much as needed.'

70

I realized I couldn't argue with her or stop and let her disappear into the field, so I just kept walking and walking and walking and the light didn't change anymore. It was as if we were suspended between day and night on that endless field and that nothing else was ever going to happen, that I was going to walk around the world and back again forever and ever.

Then... the moon came up. It was as if we'd gone over the corner of the earth. I didn't know if it had just been covered by clouds before, but there it appeared, large, silver and crystal clear in front of us. A giant gibbous moon. And in the distance something sparkled in the moonlight.

'There! There's Puddle!' she said and started walking faster, her tiny feet moving like she had a small, magical engine inside. Well, as it happened, we got to Puddle and that's exactly what Puddle was. A puddle. Puddle the puddle. I was dreadfully tired so I sat down by it and started laughing. Puddle the puddle. This was really happening to me.

'See, we got to Puddle. Now you have to go swimming.'

She said it in her normal tone so I knew she was serious. I stopped laughing.

'What do you mean swim? This is a puddle!'

'You're saying that like it's a bad thing. I know Puddle is a puddle.'

'Well how can I swim in it then?'

'Try and see.'

Swim in a puddle. Well, it couldn't be more unusual than meeting a fairy, walking across an endless field suspended in time or watching birds learn their song. So I took off my worn out shoes and looked at the puddle. The water was so clear you could count the blades of grass on the bottom. I got up on my feet and touched the water with one of my fingers. Ripples spread out wide. First one, then two, then five and then more and more as though the water was vibrating. The ground itself started to shake, and as I tried to keep my balance I tripped on one of my shoes and fell into the water. And fell and fell and fell in the water.

I just kept falling down with something as fine as silk sliding around me. My heart beat faster than it ever had, but my mind had stopped. I could hear a faint sound, like I was making music as I was falling through the silk. Only there was no silk or anything else for that matter. I could only see strands of light like lightning around me, once in a while, and I felt something like a breeze or a current from below. I closed my eyes again and realized that I would soon wake up somewhere and the little girl will be there and we will go home. I stretched out my hands and they touched something. First discretely, then more and more clearly. It felt like rock and, when I dared to look, my eyes were filled with the sight of a tall, white mountain. There were white cliffs all around me and I seemed to be resting on some sort of peak, because I could see clouds gathering below my feet.

'You touched the song. We have to go where you can sing it, now. Home.'

'We're almost there, aren't we?'

'Yes. We are. Follow me!'

CLIMBING THE MAGIC MOUNTAIN

I couldn't make out what kind of rock the mountain was made out of. When I touched it, it would remain on my fingers like chalk but in the distance it seemed to glow like marble. I came to the conclusion that it must be some type of limestone, but just as the thought entered my mind I heard the little girl's voice.

'Why are you talking silly?'

'I didn't say anything.'

'It really doesn't matter what the mountain is made out of. We must get home and that requires no talking.'

'But... I was only talking to myself. You could hear my thoughts all along?'

'No. Only after we met Puddle. You started talking louder because you touched the song, so your song is braver now and wants to come out.'

'My song is braver?'

'Yes, the song knows we are getting closer to home.'

I proceeded to be silent, inhale deeply and take a good look around. Where was I?

'We are on the magic mountain' she said. 'We have to start climbing. Home is at the top of the mountain.'

Well, of course, when on a mountain, whatever you seek seems to be at the top.

73

'How do we climb?' I thought, looking at the smooth, steep walls. 'There's nothing to grab a hold of or set foot on.'

'We have to build an umbrella.'

'An umbrella? We, the two of us, here on this empty rock, have to make an umbrella?'

'Yes. We can use my dress.'

I realized then that her dress had changed and was made of twigs. They were white so I imagined they were birch. However, I still had a hard time figuring out how to make an umbrella out of twigs.

'We will knit them,' she quickly said, obviously reading my thoughts.

'With what?'

'With your two hairpins.'

It struck me at that moment that after what seemed to be days of walking and falling down a magic puddle, my hair was still perfectly in place.

'Well, fine then. Can you knit?'

'Yes. All fairies can knit. We teach spiders how to make spider webs.'

'Good. Show me how, then.' I said, taking out my hairpins and handing them to her.

She sat down on the chalk like surface, pulled out two ends of thread from her wooden dress and started to knit with the exact same delicacy and speed with which a spider spins his web.

'Wait, you have slow down so I can understand.'

'No, I don't. Try it.'

So I sat down, pulled out my own two ends of thread, took the pins and... Glared at them.

'Well, go ahead.'

'How?!'

'Move your hands.'

'How?!'

'Just move them. If you believe that you can knit you will knit.'

I smiled to myself again considering how easy my life would be if everything worked out just like that. Then I figured that if I could reach a magic mountain, I could do anything, so I started getting the twigs closer together and swirling them one around the other and before you know it I was knitting like there was no tomorrow.

'The world is strange in proving things to us,' I thought.

The little girl proceeded to knit using two sturdier twigs she'd taken from her own dress. Our wooden thread seemed to be endless and, after a few hours of knitting, though my hands were chapped and sore, I had knit myself one cool-looking umbrella.

'Now we tie the umbrellas to each of our right hands with a thread... And throw it into the clouds.'

After knitting wood on a magic mountain, that seemed like a perfectly reasonable thing to do, so I went along. We each had an umbrella to match our size. I tossed the mushroom shaped wooden construction into mid air and, as gravity would have it, it fell and fell, through the clouds until we could no longer see it.

'What now?'

'We wait for the umbrella to come back.'

'How on earth is the umbrella going to come back?'

'Well, on earth it wouldn't. We, however, are not there. We have strong winds here. Let's wait.'

So we did and I tried my best to keep from thinking how silly all this was – Puddle the puddle and the granny-like activities and the short, mysterious sentences. I knew she could hear me think and I wanted in no way to do the faintest bit of harm to this creature, but my mind just swooped me off my feet. Only, after feeling swooped for a moment, I realized it was not my mind that did it and that I had been so unbelievably self-absorbed that I didn't realize... We were flying. The wind blew from below into our umbrellas and they shot up into the air, pulling us after them.

The little girl was laughing happily and around her everything seemed to be golden and joyful, though I could only make out passing cliffs, clouds and every once in a while what seemed to be giant birds made of ash. I stretched my arms out and felt wonderfully alive for a long, deep moment. Then... I started falling.

'Aaaaaaaaaa! Heeeeeeeelp!' I got to yell before being pulled vigorously up for a second, at the end of which I proceeded to descend slowly. Our umbrellas had turned into parachutes. The little girl was drifting down slowly and smoothly right next to me and I felt like I loved her.

'Where are we going?' I asked.

'Back to the top of the mountain. But look! Look up!' she said and as I did my world became all the more wonderful. I think we were somewhere very high above the ground or the sky because it looked we were so close to the stars that their light fell warmly around us like a rainbow. Pink, gold and blue light was somehow suspended in mid-air. The
beauty of it filled my eyes with tears.

'Thank you!' I whispered and she burst into soft, joyous laughter.

'Look down now! We're close to home,' she said, and with her voice I heard the sound of music coming from above.

Below us there was actually... A house. A small wooden cabin, covered in moss, with a chimney that sent little tufts of smoke up. It looked warm, cozy and friendly. I could imagine myself having hot chocolate on a cold day sitting on its old wooden porch.

We landed right in front of it and walked slowly to open the door. The room was small but perfect: the fire was burning in the stove and there was a large and comfy looking armchair in front of it. The walls were covered in what seemed to be story books, save for one that had cooking instruments hung all over it. Under one of the windows, close to the fire, there was a little, cozy bed.

'We are here and I have to go. And you are tired and you have to go to sleep.'

'Are you leaving? Don't you want cocoa?'

'I have to go help a child that is lost in the woods. I am a forest fairy. I help children who need to find home .You are here now, so I have to go.'

I felt a deafening sadness as she just turned around and went outside. She closed the door and when I ran to open it, she'd disappeared.

I went and sat on the bed and started hugging the pillow. I wished she would have stayed for cocoa. I stretched out on the clean sheets and immediately fell sound asleep. Can you guess where I woke up?

THE LIZARD PRINCE AND THE FIRE FROG

Part I

The prince went out every morning, earlier than anyone, to climb the sharpest white boulder by the edge of the river. He ran to get to the top before the frame of the sun could be seen above the dusty clouds in the morning horizon. He grabbed on to the knife-like edges with his long claws, embodying an ease that had made him famous among his lizard clan. He was a natural born climber, and he had crawled up every tree or rock that stood in his way since he had been a hatchling.

But the prince would not see the end of his journey that day. No sooner had he crossed the shallow river than the ground split open before him with a great roar and orange flames shot up like burning snakes that cracked and hissed. They lasted only for a moment, if at all. By the time the prince had come to his senses, nothing was left on the smooth dirt but a crooked, ugly old frog with bulging eyes.

'What sorcery is this?' the prince asked. 'Are you a conjurer? Why are you in my path?' The frog lay motionless on the dirt, croaking away as if the prince wasn't even there. The stranger had such a coldness about him that the prince forgot all about his boulder and said a little prayer to himself, that he would get home safely and see his mother and father again.

'You don't seem like a bad soul' the frog then started, out of nowhere. Its gaze was still fixed on the boulder and its eyes looked so empty that the prince imagined the nothingness inside them reaching out to swallow him. 'You climb this wretched boulder every day to challenge yourself. But what do you really know about challenge? What do you really know about coming head to head with fear, and doubt, and destiny?'

The prince had no answer. He stared at the grass between his claws. He had thought it himself. He was not a warrior. He was not a commander. He was barely anything. The spoiled son of an old, respected king. Completely unprepared for taking his father's place. His father. The great defender of the Valley of Green.

'I can make you what you wish to become. I can make you great and powerful and wise.'

'But there is a price, I assume?'

'There is always a price, Prince. A small one to pay for such an offering.'

Let's hear it, then.

'You have to find a way to turn me back into a man. And until you do, you will be bound to me.'

'Like a servant?'

'You will not have to do chores for me, like a servant, but you will not decide anything by yourself. I shall be your counselor in everything. Everything.'
'So I will be a king with no power of his own?'

'You will be the most beloved king there ever was.' When he said it, the wizard frog conjured things as the prince would have them before him. The prince saw himself leading an army to victory and being cheered on by all his men. He saw himself defending the city from a swarm of locusts and saving each and every one of his fellow lizards.

'Very well. I do not know exactly where this will lead. But anything is better than living like a spoiled brat without any merit. I accept your challenge. I will serve you and you will turn me into a warrior, a conqueror and the defender of my people. So be it.'

The prince had just finished his words, when the frog disappeared with a giant puff of smoke. The fog was so thick that it darkened everything, causing the prince to start coughing and gasping for breath. He ran to find air but the darkness had no end. He fell to the ground. When his knees touched the dirt, he suddenly felt that he was being pulled down with tremendous force, as if a whirlwind was dragging him inside. It lasted only a moment, but when he opened his eyes, scared, with his heart pounding and his head burning, he was in his bed, in the castle dormitory.

Outside a fiery red dawn was breaking. He looked out of the window to see the shadow of the boulder he always climbed. It look just like a hunched old frog, with bulging eyes.

THE LIZARD PRINCE AND THE FIRE FROG

Part II

'A nightmare. It was just a nightmare' the prince thought. 'I didn't do that. I haven't laid my life at stake for the promise of an old frog. Oh, dear me... It felt so real. But it was nothing. Nothing.' The prince turned in his bed and fell fast asleep again. At the last moment, had he been paying attention, he would have heard the slightest voice in his head saying: 'You have my permission to fall sleep.' But he had not been, and the morning fell upon him without any warning.

'Get up! Get up! Get UP!' the voice screamed. The prince jumped out of his bed, grabbed his sword and pointed it threateningly to the door. But not a moment passed before he staggered to his feet and started muttering gibberish. 'Open your eyes at once!' the voice sounded again. Indeed, the prince did, as, despite his gestures, he had yet to wake up.

'Now hurry to meet your father. He's waiting for you, he has something to tell you.'

The prince didn't pause to think. We rarely do when we hear the voice inside our heads. Maybe he took it for intuition. Maybe for another dream. But he rushed to the study where his father usually wrote long letters in the mornings. His father was still a powerful man, despite his age. He was perhaps the most beloved king of his dynasty. He was the first king to abolish the slavery of tree frogs and, in so doing, end the great civil war. This had happened years before the prince was born but the memory of it was very much awake in the heart of the people that had started to know prosperity again after long decades of sending their loved ones to the Bloody Valley, never to return again.

'I do not have good news, my son. I'm glad you came to see me so early. Do you remember your military training?'
'Perhaps better than anything, father.'

'Good. You will need it. And you will be leaving us for a while, son.'

'Where is it your will that I go, father?'

'To the north. To the kingdom of the tree frogs. Their king just died without an heir and a swarm of locusts, sensing weakness, is at their gates. You will go to defend them.'

'I will leave as the next dawn breaks.'

'Good. Let us talk for a while now, son. It will be some time before we do it again.' the king said, closing the door to his study.

THE LIZARD PRINCE AND THE FIRE FROG

The prince left his father's study in a trance. His legs took him to the drawing room, where the giant windows opened upon the river valley. The fog was clearing from above the water. The prince gazed at it with his mind wandering. He turned his head to the gleaming boulder he used to climb and in a moment the memory of his dream fell upon him with all its weight.

'The old frog... The old wizard. What did I dream? Could it be true? This war... Out of nowhere. Is it real? Am I still dreaming? This forest, as old as it is... Has it ever seen a lizard as foolish as me?'

The next day the prince left to defend the tree frogs and their kingdom without a king. He was welcomed at their city gates with cheers. 'Hooray for the son of King Atlas!' they called. The prince felt petty and meek.

'Will I be able to defend these creatures? These mothers who bring their babies to see me? These boys who run in the street and skip stones in the water? Will they be alive in two days time when the locusts invade? Will I rise to the challenge? Or will I fail and make both mine and their parents weep? Stories of great victories are easier heard than lived. I am scared for my life.'

In the morning of the invasion a great wind howled from the west. It was cold and harsh, like a giant throwing needles getting ready to swallow the earth whole. The sky was a dark, silvery gray. The swarm of locusts appeared on the horizon like an eruption of tar, rising up from the ground. 'There are so many of them.' the prince thought. 'And so few of us.'

He summoned the fire blowers up on the city walls. The catapults were aligned on the streets. Every creature capable of heavy work had built catapults. There were hundreds of them, each loaded with the thickest, stickiest spider web in the forest.

The swarm of locusts grew larger and larger. In moments it seemed to cover the entire horizon. The prince measured the distance with his spy glass.

Catapults reeeady!' he called. 'Aim! Fire!'

A rain of silk lifted from the castle and moved above the field It reached the tower of tar and poured over it, white and fine, like snow. The horizon grew whiter and whiter, as if the earth was absorbing the darkness. The clear, white sky lasted barely a moment. For no sooner had the first wave of attack been stopped, than another rose behind it. Taller, darker and angrier. Like none that had ever been seen.

Part IV

The siege lasted for seven nights and days. Save for the children, no one in the castle had slept at all. The mothers boiled tar, kept the fires burning for the fire blowers and prepared food and bandages for the soldiers. Boys who were too young to fight made bombs of tar and flint and carried them up the walls.

The prince had been up on the wall for every moment of the assault. With his spider web bow he had shot down over four hundred locusts, sometimes five at a time. The fire blowers looked at him with a form of respect he had yet to encounter in his own life. He recognized it from when he visited the barracks with his father. It was not mere obedience or the homage of royalty. It was the admiration of strength and valor, the sense that made soldiers follow a commander blindly into battle, knowing that he, in turn, would die for each and every one of them. This had kept him fighting along his men, without pause. Only on the seventh day, at noon, as he stopped for a drink of water, he laid his forehead on a sack of arrows. He'd barely touched the cloth when his eyes closed and he fell into a deep sleep.

He dreamt that he had left the castle through a secret passageway that led into the forest. He ran for hours until the web of trees was so thick that the sunlight barely shone through. He could only see three feet in front of him, yet he ran guided by the voice in his head: 'Go meet the Spider Queen!' it said. 'Go and she will save you.' So he pressed on, until a beam of white light shot straight by him.

He stopped shaking on his feet and called: 'I am the son of King Atlas! I have come to see the Queen!' and hoped with all his might that he would live to see sunlight again. In a moment, the leaves above him started to move, twitching and squirming. As another beam of light shone through, he noticed with horror that he couldn't see one tree branch, only layers and layers of web and the countless legs of black spiders. He almost lost his breath when thread started to fall around him but, as he struggled to keep from fainting, he saw that the spiders were building a ladder. Descending upon it, straight from the roof of the forest, came a single, white spider.

'What message does the King send us?'

'I come on my own behalf. As the King of the tree frogs.'

'I see. So I imagine you want my army to defend you from the locust invasion. Which I will consider if... you can tell me why we, forest spiders, do not have any allies.'

The prince felt his heart pounding in his head. In his desperation, he had not asked himself about the very thing known of spiders. They had never waged a war and they had never been attacked. When the peoples of the valley were fighting for freedom, it was as if they never existed.

'You look confused. The King's son should have come better prepared. But let me tell you, since you are here. It is because everyone fears us. Not one locust has ever set foot in our forest, so why should we care who lives or dies in your petty wars?'

'So it would all end,' the prince thought. He'd left his soldiers on the walls for nothing. He was ready to bow his eyes when the voice in his head called: 'A king does not bow his head! Look into her eyes and give her what she wants!'

'But I don't know... I...'

'Your army is starving!' the prince suddenly called. 'Without this war you die. The locusts would not come here but you have to attack them. There is nothing left near this forest but us and them, and there are too few of us to keep you alive!'

'So you are your father's son. Very well. My army and I will come with you. We will travel above the trees. Artax will take you on his back. We leave now.'

The prince felt himself being sucked into a whirlwind again and opened his eyes to see the sack of arrows under his head. He jumped to his feet and called out his men. He would be missing for a few hours, he said, and urged them to fight onward. He donned his cloak and ran to the secret passageway. It was there, just as he had dreamt. It would not be long until he returned with a new army.

THE LIZARD PRINCE AND THE FIRE FROG

The spiders stormed the field with such fury that the locusts, completely unprepared, were defeated before nightfall. Most fell prisoner, trapped under the sticky layers of web. The spiders wrapped them in giant cocoons and dragged them slowly to the forest. The sight of it sent shivers down the prince's spine. On the other side of the city, the tree frogs had started to clean up the remnants of the siege.

The prince was sitting in front of his window, as if waiting for something to happen, when the floor started to shake. A cold wind blew the windows open and the moonlight cast a familiar shadow on his wall.

'It's my father, isn't it? I just realized it now. My father made you like this. That's why you came to me. You need me to undo my father's work. So you're turning me into him!'

'How unexpected of you, young prince. It is your father, yes. And only you or he can save me.'

'Why not him? Why would I save you if he made you like this?'

'Because I changed. But he won't see me. He hasn't seen me since it happened. We used to be friends, you see. I promised to be his ally in the great war. Only my army never came. I left him to fight alone. So he placed a curse on me, in anger. And here I stand.'

'Why did you not do as you had promised?'

'My council forbade it. I was young then, a new king on an old throne that I did not deserve. Just like you felt before we met. They didn't listen to me so I could not take the army.'
'So why not tell my father?'

89

'I was too ashamed. So I chose to fulfill my promise now. With you. So that maybe then he would forgive me. Will you help me prince? Will you speak to your father? Will you be my ally?'

'I... You saved my people. I have been here for merely weeks, but these have become my people. So yes, I will speak to my father. He is a good man.'

'Thank you.' the frog barely said, and disappeared as if into thin air.

The prince sat in front of his window, gazing at the field. For the first time in his life, he felt like a king.

THE PIRATE'S TALE

'Saaandy! Saaaandy!' Tommy yelled at the top of his lungs, right in front of Sandy's gate.

'She's not here, Tommy, she went fishing with Martha!' her mother said out of an open window. She was wearing the orange apron she always wore when she baked cookies. Tommy thought Sandy's mother looked like a princess. A princess who made the most delicious cookies in the world.

'Thank you, Mrs. Watsooon!' he yelled and ran off towards the meadow. 'I am going fishing! I am going fishing! I am going fishing!' Tommy merrily repeated as he skipped along the way. Passing by Mr. Brown's house he imagined, as always, that his wooden fence used to be a war barricade. Maybe even Mr. Brown used to be a warrior before he became a fisherman. That's when he realized... He didn't have a fishing rod! Where could he find one?

'Mr. Brooooown! Mr. Broooooooown! Mr. Brooooooown!'

'What?! Who's calling? Who is there? I can't see you. The gate is open, just come in.'

'Hello Mr. Brown! Could I borrow a fishing rod?'

'Well... yes, you could. Why do you need it?'

'To go fishing, Mr. Brown!'

'Yes, Tommy, I know that. But why from me and why now?'

'Sandy's by the river with Martha and they're fishing. And I want to go but I have no rod and I was near your house. So I need a rod to go fishing.'

'Ok, Tommy. But we have to go get one from my fishing cabin, in the meadow. We can go right now.'

'Great! Thank you, Mr. Brown!'

'Did your dad teach you how to fish, Tommy?'

'No, sir. My grandpa did. My daddy doesn't know how to fish. He's an engineer. He works on engines.'

'Well that's curious. I thought everyone around these parts knew how to fish. Maybe you should take your dad out fishing sometime.'

'I want to, sir, but daddy usually doesn't want to go with me. He stays at home with mommy. Mommy cooks and daddy stays in the kitchen where he has this big board and table that he draws on. He does figures and strange numbers and things. I think he must be really smart. Sometimes he explains to me how things work, and then I feel like I'm smart like he is too.'

'How old are you, Tommy?'

'8, sir. I'm going to be 9 in September. I'm a big boy now and I have to help my mommy and grandpa out in the yard and garden and such.'

'That's good thinking, Tommy.'

'Mr. Brown, why don't you have any kids?'

'Well, Tommy, that's a good question. I hope I'll have my own soon. I'm to be married this summer.'

'Really?!'

'Yes, Tommy, I'll be marrying a girl from the city.'

'Wow, a city girl! I see a few of the college girls from town when I go to school. They're almost as pretty as Sandy's mother.'

'I think this one is just about as pretty as Sandy's mother if you ask me.'

'Congratulations, Mr. Brown! But aren't you too old to get married?'

'I was engaged once before. But my sweetheart's parents wouldn't let her marry a young pirate. They thought I'd die or go to jail before I got to offer their little girl a proper life. They were probably right at the time too.'

93

'What, Mr. Brown?!' Tommy said with amazement. 'You used to be a pirate?!'

'Indeed I did, Tommy. Indeed, I did. Let's sit down by the river bank and I'll tell you all about it.'

THE PIRATE'S TALE

Part II

'See, when I was your age, Tommy, I used to live in a big city by the ocean, down south and to the west. My folks had their home right near the harbor so after school I'd hang around with some other boys around the docks. We didn't do nothing much, mostly hung around the sailors and asked them to tell us their stories. Now, one day, an old man shows up on the dock. He doesn't say anything, just looks at the sea and the boats and tears come to his eyes and then he gets on his knees and kisses the wood of the deck. First I thought he must be some crazy old man to kiss that dirty wood that everybody walked on. But, when he got up there was a fire in his eyes. See, Tommy, I realized that either the dock or the sea or the boats or all of them together meant more to that old man than I could ever dream of understanding. So, curious kid that was, instead of running along to play with my friends I went to talk to him just like you started talking to me. I said:

'Sir, why'd you kiss the dock for?'

And the old man looked at me dead serious and said:

'Because I left this here dock to go to Willow Island and came back alive to tell the story.'

'What's Willow Island?'

'Son, you don't know about Willow Island? Hell, when I was your age every kid on the coast dreamed of setting foot on it. It's a magical island where water runs backwards, up to the sky from the middle of the island and you can catch the largest sea bass you've ever laid eyes on. They also say that in those waters there's one giant green fish, the spirit of the island, that can fulfill any man's wishes if he catches him. Many have tried, and only I have come back to tell the tale.'

'You're a sailor?'

'Indeed I used to be. I'm old and gray now, but I've still got some tricks up my sleeve.'

'Can you teach me how to be a sailor?'

'Hehe!' he laughed. 'I like you, kid. Yeah, I reckon I could if you're not one to back down.'

'Never, sir! I'll do everything you say if you teach me how to be a sailor!'

So the old man accepted and took me to be his apprentice on his old, worn-out sail boat. The Gray Wolf she was called; and despite her age, she was a mighty fine boat. I remember one time we were caught in a thunderstorm out at sea. The waves hit her so hard from the side she almost laid flat on the surface of the water for what seemed to one of the longest moments of my life. The silence was deafening as she stood tilted. Suddenly there was a blinding light and a roaring thunder, and she erupted back up like she was trying to stab the storm's heart. The waters calmed down afterwards and we sailed home with the wind.

I learned to pull up the sails and steer her in clear weather and in bad winds and measure our speed and position and navigate with a map. After a couple of years next to the old man, I felt like a real sailor even if I was still no more than a boy. The old man didn't talk much, but he took an honest liking to me and promised that one day he'd show me the way to Willow Island.

Truth be told, I was happy as a boy could be. I was out at sea all day. My skin was darkened by the sun and my hands were worn from pulling on the ropes and the wood and salt water. My shirts all had holes in them that my mother would sew up. They stopped buying new ones because I just came back home with them all torn and no one but the sun could see me all day long anyways.

So one day, we headed out to sea. Further than usual. We caught a really good wind and the Wolf was just flying. I went up to the crow's nest to look for land with my spyglass, see if I could spot any. And I didn't, but I saw a ship up north. Dark and slender. Couldn't make out the flag. So I yelled out to the old man who said we should go and meet our fellow sailors. Said he's gonna teach me the courtesies of making acquaintance with another ship out at sea. Something that done properly can save a ship captain's life, he said. So we went.

We came up really close behind them. I kept my spyglass on their mast, but they weren't showing any flag. The old man had me move up behind the ship, fill the old cannon with powder and fire it, to signal the meeting.

In a few moments, the ship had started to slowly turn towards us, and suddenly we saw it. The skull and crossed bones of the Nemesis. The last and fiercest pirate ship of the sea. I remember I was so scared, I could feel my heart drumming in my ears. I'd heard stories about the Nemesis. She was built like a great white. Her mast towered threateningly above the water and she parted the waves like she had the sea's blessing to roam it. Her captain, De Ville, invoked terror into the heart of every seaman I'd ever known. He was said to be four hundred years old and the most cunning, cruel and cut-throat seaman to ever sail the seven seas.

Part III

The Nemesis turned toward us and, for a few seconds, there was dead silence. Then the roaring of cannons started. One after the other. Boom! Boom! Boom! I could hear them from all directions and just stood there paralyzed in fear. The old man hadn't taught me what to do if the ship was attacked. No ship had been attacked in those waters for over 25 years. But through the rumbling, I hear his voice.

'Load the cannon, kid! We're not gonna go out standing still, are we?! Let's see who gets sunk first!'

So I started loading the powder with my bare hands. I stuffed it down the barrel, and as I saw the old man running towards me I lit a match and fired, without a second thought. The blast threw me back a couple of feet and almost knocked me out cold. I lay there for a moment, trying to figure out if I was still alive. I grabbed on to some rope to get back on my feet, just to see if I could still use 'em. My muscles hurt and my heart was pumping in my chest. My head felt two sizes bigger. With my legs shaking I stood up and looked at the Nemesis. I could see the mast swaying, and thought I must be seeing things. But then something happened that I will remember for the rest of my life. The mast swayed one final time and fell down with a loud thump and a giant splash which covered half the deck in water. It pulled the sails down with it, causing them to drag across the deck. I could hear yelling and the realization of what I had done dawned on me. My eyes opened wide, growing to the size of tennis balls, as I stared at the stump left behind. The old man was looking at me, awestruck.

'Kid! What in God's name did you do?!'

And me, with my legs still shaking and my voice seizing up, could only put up kind of a smirk and say: 'I done shot their mast down, sir!'

'You're either the luckiest or the darnedest shooter I ever met!

Now stop the damn grinning and load that there cannon again.' So I started pushing and shoving to aim the cannon for the second time in my life, unable to even understand how I had done it the first time when the thing is so heavy that my hands could barely move it an inch here and there. My mind was roaring with memories of my mom and dad, how they were waiting for me and how I may never come back, my mother crying and yelling that she should have never let me become a sailor.

I almost burst into tears but then, all of a sudden, I was shot off my feet into a pile of ropes nearby. I hear a loud crack, water hits my face and the ship sways and tilts and I feel seasick. I can't make out anything through the smoke and I yell out for the old man. I covered my eyes with my hands and try to force myself not to cry. I told myself that I had to be strong like a sailor and get up, but I couldn't get the ropes off my legs. I felt like I was spiraling down a drain and that I would never come back. When I finally had the heart to open my eyes, I looked up and saw it. A giant, dark shadow, sharp like a spear. The bow of the Nemesis. She'd sailed right into us.

I pushed myself up on the ropes and looked around to see the Wolf is almost torn in half. Dark shadows are coming down the ropes and I started to pray that they let me live. Soon enough, one of them grabbed me by the scruff of my neck, dragged me across the deck and shoved me into a sack. I fainted.

THE PIRATE'S TALE

When I woke up... There was no dungeon, no prison, no chains and misery, like I had expected. None of that. I was in a sumptuous ship cabin, in a soft warm bed. Next to me stood a large silver tray, filled with food. My stomach *started rumbling, as I realized I was as hungry as a pack of wolves. I started grabbing food off of the tray and eating it with my hands, hoping that nobody would walk in and see me.

But sure enough, someone did. He was tall. But I mean really tall, like he was a man and a half. And he had these big, dark eyes that could see right through you. When he looked at me I could feel my heart jumping up into my throat. But he didn't look like a pirate. Or at least, not how I imagined pirates. He looked more like a noble man. Like a duke or something. He was dressed in a dark blue frock coat and vest. He was holding an ebony cane with a silver plated handle, engraved with willow leaves.

I had a piece of fish in my hand and crumbs all over the front of my shirt. He looked at me and I felt ashamed, but to my surprise he smiled. Not a cold or disgusted smile either, but a warm, honest, "I like you" smile. So I managed to close my mouth and put down the food.

'Don't mind me, just carry on eating. I only wanted to see if you were alright. Do you mind if I sit down next to you? Would you like me to come back when you're done eating?'

I could not bring myself to say anything.

'You seem fearful. Please don't be. You're safe. No one will hurt you on this ship. I am the Captain.'

With my heart still in my throat I managed to get out three words. 'Captain De Ville?'

'That would be me, yes. So you've heard of me. Hence the fear, probably.'

'You're a pirate.'

'I am. And you are...'

'A sailor.'

'Well, I'm also a sailor. Just a certain kind of sailor. You have a name, sailor?'

'Peter.' I said. That isn't my name, but it was the first one that came to mind. Truth be told, I liked the man the first moment I saw him. He was a gentleman. I didn't want to look stupid in front of a gentleman.

'Hello, Peter. I am Elijah. When you're done eating please visit me in my office cabin.'

After he left, I started inspecting the room. A desk stood right by the bed, with a beautiful old map spread out on top of it. In one corner, I could make out my home land. In another...there was Willow Island. I wanted to read the way there but there were symbols on the map that I'd never seen before. At first I tried to read them. But soon enough I realized that if I closed my eyes, even for an instant, they would change into something else. After a while, I gave up and decided to visit the Captain.

I knocked at the door and he called me in. I noticed that there was no bed in this cabin. Only maps, compasses, a few sextants, a back staff, spyglasses, hourglasses, a nocturnal and even a ring dial. The walls and shelves were filled with them, like the room was a museum of navigational instruments. In the center stood an ebony desk with chairs, all of them engraved with willow leaves.

'Sit down, Peter. I want us to talk about how you took down my mast. Don't worry, I'm not angry or upset. I just want to know how in God's name you did it. I fought hundreds of battles and the Nemesis hasn't ever been damaged. Up until now.'

'I don't know, sir. I didn't do nothing special. I just loaded the cannon and shot.'

'Who taught you to shoot the cannon?'

'No one did, sir. It was the first time I fired a cannon. I think it was darn luck, is what it was. I have no idea how I did it.'

'I see. So how'd you get on that ship?'

'I've been sailing with the old man since I was a boy. I want to know what happened to him.'

'We took him aboard and then dropped him off in a life boat, near the shore, a few days later. He's alive and well, don't worry.'

'How can I be sure?'

'I am a pirate of my word. I don't harm old men. Look, Peter, I want you to be part of my crew. I figure any man who's lucky enough to do me harm might as well be on my side. What do you think?'

'You want me to be a pirate?'

'Yes. I will teach you how to sail but you have to promise to be completely loyal. You must never lie to me, never do anything to harm the Nemesis or its crew, you do everything in your power to keep it alive and afloat.'

'I already know how to sail.'

'No you don't, Peter. You know how to sail like a man. I'm going to teach you to sail like the spirit of the water. You'll never drown, your ship will never sink, your men will always listen to you and you'll become a myth. Like me. You'll be able to travel around the world if you want, the sea and the stars will take you there. You'll see places no sailor has ever seen.'

'But I don't want to be a pirate.'

'Well, I'm afraid that's not an option. You are on the Nemesis and you will stay on the Nemesis and as this is a pirate ship, you are a pirate. We don't pillage, plunder, steal or kill. We protect Willow Island. That is what we do. Sometimes when we do it we sink other ships so they call us pirates. That is not important. Our name is not important. Who we are is. I am a Captain and you will be trained to be a pilot and my second. You will become a myth, Peter.'

'So what if I say no?'

'You won't.'

'What if I still say it?'

'We'll leave you like the old man and when you wake up you won't remember any of this. You'll live a normal life, like your parents and their parents and nothing like this will ever happen to you again. But I'm getting tired. I don't ask twice. Will you join my crew or won't you?'

'I will.'

'Things are as they should be. Go see the ship now, Peter. Forfax is waiting for you outside. He will be your guide. He is now my second. When the time is right you will take his place. Learn everything from him.'

I walked out and, sure enough, there was Forfax. He was tall, though not quite like the captain, and he had large, round spectacles and white hair. He looked like a scientist.

'I hear your name is Peter. I am Forfax. I am your guide. As such, you can ask me anything. But, first of all, I have to tell you something that you wouldn't think of asking. On this ship everyone has a special skill. A sort of power to understand and do something. Mine is astronomy. The crew only consists of seven people, including yourself. I...'

'Must I have a skill to be here?'

'It's not polite to interrupt. I think so. The captain has issued no rule on it, but it seems to be the habit of the place.'

'How could you sail a ship this big with just six people?'

'The ship does a lot of the work herself.'

'What?'

'Please ask more precise questions.'

'How does the ship do anything?'

'She is, after all, a magical ship. She also has a... master, if you will.'

'The captain?'

'No. He is her commander. Her master is her architect, the man who built the Nemesis. Phoebus. You will meet him later. There is not much human sailing done on this ship.'

'But how can she sail? Who positions the sails? Who steers?'

'The captain decides where to go, but she steers herself. Phoebus manages everything else. The captain decides where, he decides how and she gets there.'

'That's impossible.'

'I think "magical" is a much more suitable word. The Nemesis is magical, as are the people on it.'

'You have magical powers? Does that mean I have magical powers?'

'No. We just have a magical understanding of things.'

'What is that?'

'We... understand how things come together. When the wind blows, it blows in a certain way for a reason. If you know why, you can either use it, change it or ignore it, depending on where you want to arrive.'

'Will you teach me that?'

'You will learn it as you live here with us. First of all, though, you have to sail us to Willow Island.'

'But how can I sail there if the ship sails by herself?'
'You have to make your will her will.'

'How?'

'I can't explain, but you will do it, the captain has no doubt.
Now, we will go to the bow. You have to meet the rest of the crew.
We're supposed to set sail under your direction as soon as
possible.'

Part VI

I had no idea how to do what was asked of me. I stood on the bowsprit, looking at the stem slicing through the sea. My thoughts wandered home. I remembered everything that the old man had taught me. And to what avail? I couldn't sail the Nemesis that way. So I sat down on the ancient wooden floor and started talking to her.

I told her all sorts of things. That I was just lucky to be there. That I had no special skill, other than my sheer fortune. That I was ashamed and wanted to become a good second for the Captain. Though I feared I'd never be as smart as Forfax. I asked her to take me to Willow Island... so I wouldn't have to leave the ship. I also asked her to keep me alive so I can see my parents and the old man once again.

After a while, when I finally looked up, I saw a beautiful, shattering sunset. Like someone had peeled off the skin of the sky. I felt tiny drops of water hitting my face and took in the salty smell of the ocean. And that's when I saw it. A shard of blue cutting through the cloth of the sunset, from the bottom all the way up, where the sky turns to black. I remembered what the old man had told me. Water, running backwards, from the ground up towards the sky. Under it, I can make out a speck of brown and green. We were heading to Willow Island.

'Land Ho!' I call. Only I hear no footsteps or cheering. I turn around... And there he was again.

'How'd I do that, Forfax?'

'Same way you knocked the mast down, probably. You know how. You're just not used to thinking about it. Let's go to the berth deck.'

I thought I was finally meeting the other crew, so I followed Forfax in silence, thinking about what I was going to say.

'Where is everyone else? You mentioned four more people.'

'They're here. They just have no business with you. When they do, you'll meet them.'

'Here where?'

'Here in this room and everywhere else. On the ship. Now here, look at this map. This is Willow Island.'

It was the same map I'd seen in my room earlier. The lines were still moving.

'The signs are changing. And I can't read this... this... whatever it is. I don't know the language.'

'You're not looking at it properly. You're looking at it as if it owed it to you to show you the way. But it will not do so if it is not indeed your way. If your path is set to Willow Island and it's not important what gets you there, the map will just as well show you the way. If not, it won't.'

'That's ridiculous. It's a map. It's supposed to show the way whether I have to get there or not!'

'Whether you agree or not with how things work here makes no difference whatsoever. Nothing will change. I will leave you with that thought. When you're done call for Phoebus.'

He turned around and left without another word. I sat on the chair and held my head in my hands, feeling abandoned and alone. The map was stretched out across the table in front of me, so I glanced at it from time to time.

The lines were moving faster than before. They began in the south and moved in a block, towards the northeast. After going about three quarters of the way, they made a turn to the southwest and started moving faster. In a few moments, they turned yet again, only this time heading back east. This led them right to the center of the map, where they seemed to just drift for a while. Then the cycle was repeated.

Somehow, the pattern seemed familiar. It was like the flight of birds when they gathered to fly south. It was not the flight itself that I was trying to remember though, but why they did it. It was like they were following an unseen path. That was when I realized... It was the wind. They were moving with the wind.

The lines on the map showed a current and, most likely, safe passage to the island. The strange letters weren't even writing. They were drawings of rocks and cliffs the boat had to avoid. I turned around to call for Phoebus. But when I saw what was behind me I jumped back, fell over the chair, and started yelling. I was scared out of my senses.

Behind me I saw a giant, dark figure. I thought it was going to attack me. Had it decided to, there was no way I could fight it. It was twice as tall as me and three foot wide. After I fell backwards, it started to walk towards me slowly. When it got closer, it leaned towards me and extended its hand.

It was Phoebus. His skin was dark, he was dressed in black and his hands were covered in black grease. He was even taller than the Captain.

'Peter? Are you alright? I didn't want to scare you... Forfax just told me you need me. I'm Phoebus.' He had a warm and honest voice.

'You found the way to the island, so now you have to sail us there. The way is too complicated for the Nemesis to handle all by herself. Besides, now we don't have no main mast either, so we have to be really careful. The foremast should do for this journey, but once we get to the island we're fixin' the Nemesis good as new.'

'Phoebus, I've never sailed a ship with no mast before.'

'I have a few times, before I built the Nemesis. Don't worry, she'll do just fine. Now let's get going. We got to get to the island by morning.'

So we sailed. It was as if every little line on the map was branded into my head. I knew exactly where to go and what to do, like I'd been there a hundred times before. When the sun started to rise we were so close to the island that I could make out the shapes of the trees. I could see rivers running from the top of the island towards the sea-shore, tens of them, and the blue torrent still climbing to the sky. Forfax had mentioned I had to meet the spirit of the island. But what for? I went down to the Captain's cabin and knocked.

'I know why you came to see me. I can't fully answer your question right now. What I can tell you is that every man on this ship had to pass a test to be admitted in the crew. You are no exception.'

'How do you always know what I want to say?'

'Forfax told you about how every man has a skill. He understands the stars, seas and winds. I understand thoughts. I can't read thoughts or hear them, I just can tell what people want, hope and expect.'

'Is that why you're the captain?'

'Sometimes I think so. Truth is, who can tell? You have to go back to the deck now. Alistair is waiting for you. He'll go with you to the island. The rest of us will wait for you here.'

'Is the island dangerous?'

'Depends on the man treading on it. You should know that better than anybody. Hurry now.'

Outside the door I met Alistair. He looked slender and sharp, like an elf. He only said that he was in charge of defending the ship and its crew. Nothing more. We sailed towards the island in a small boat in complete silence. We hoisted the boat up onto the beach. Alistair proceeded to lead me to a path between the trees. It zig-zagged across the rivers. We had to jump from rock to rock, holding on to the lower willow branches or using poles to steady ourselves. I could hear birds all around us, but after over two hours on the island, I had yet to see a single one.

It was early morning. The sunlight was clear and transparent, illuminating the mess of green all around us. The water was full of willow branches and leaves, and sparkled gold and silver. Green lizards were scurrying under rocks. I felt like I'd dreamed about this place when I was a child. We walked all day. The path went higher and higher along the river valleys and the ground was getting steeper.

When the sun started to set, we walked into a clearing. It was beautiful and silent, like nothing I'd ever seen. You couldn't hear the birds or the water there. It seemed to be suspended in time. In the middle of the clearing stood a strange formation of rocks – a round, larger one that looked like a table and seven smaller ones, like chairs.

'I will wait for you here.' Alistair said. 'The way was difficult but you did not complain or stop and nothing else came to stop us. This means you have a good heart, a heart the island chooses to protect. You will go through those trees and after a short climb you will meet the spirit. Go now.'

I felt calm and at ease and climbed without rush or concern. I knew that, whatever happened, arriving there was more than any man could hope for. When I hoisted myself up a rocky ledge and was able to see the water running up towards the sky, a mere six feet away from me, I could ask for no more. I turned around, sat on the ledge and looked at the sunset.

'Dreadfully beautiful, isn't it?' a female voice said. 'Can I sit with you?'

'Of course. Yes, it is. The sunsets are even better here than they are on the mainland. The water turns red, white and gold. I love that. It's as if the sky turns upside down so you feel like you're sailing on it. But I noticed this water here never changes color. Why?'

'Well, this water here is the essence of the world. It doesn't have to change.'

'And you are the spirit of the island.'

'I am. And I am said to fulfill wishes.'

'And do you really do that?'

'It depends. There are two types of people. Those who fight to fulfill their own wishes and those who don't. The first ones I can't do much for. The others either wish for things that shouldn't belong to them, or just don't try hard enough. So I can't really help them either. It is not the way of the spirit to provide for the lazy or greedy. So I am actually pretty much of no use to anybody.'

'That makes sense. Do you know what I'm doing here?'

'I do. You are here because you wanted to make this journey. You wanted to meet Captain de Ville, sail the Nemesis and reach Willow Island. So you did it. There is nothing more I can do for you.'

'But wasn't that just luck? I didn't even know how to fire a cannon.'

'Luck comes to people for a reason. You once said to the old man that you're not one to back down. That has something to do with it. Now you have to go back to Alistair. Together you'll get back to the ship and set sail. You'll meet the rest of the crew and become the captain's second.'

'But what will happen to Forfax?'

'Forfax wants to go home. The Nemesis will sail forever but the people on it have hopes and dreams outside a lifetime of sailing. One day you will leave too. You will want a home on the ground with a yard and children running around it. And that will be good.'

'I will see my home again?'
'You will. Now go back to Alistair. I have nothing more to say.'

I went back and everything was as she said. And now here I am, telling you this story.

'Mr. Brown... It's the best story I've ever heard in my entire life. Can we please be friends? Will you tell me more stories?'

'Yes, Tommy, we can. I will.'

'Can I tell the other kids this story?'

'Yes, you can. And if they come and ask me I'll tell them it's true. And we can go fishing anytime you like.'

'Do we go home now?'

'Yes, we go home now. It's getting dark.'

THE BOY WHO CHASED THE SUNSET

Part I

'I think this is it. Yup. We are so stuck here!'

'Come ooon! No, we're not!'

'Danny, there's a field of corn in front of us. The road just stops. Where do we go from here?'

'We keep going. Follow me!'

So off he went through the corn, with Rosie following him.

'What are you doing!? Danny! Let's go back! Let's go home!'

'Look, if you want to go, stop whining. If not, turn around. All I know is I'm not stopping.'

Now where were they going you might wonder? Well, it's a really lovely story. When Danny was a boy, he got lost in the forest. The magical forest next to his village. He was chasing a fox that always came into his yard and looked at him, like it wanted to say something. Then, after a few moments of inquisitive staring, it went back under the fence and into the forest. Danny became more and more curious until he couldn't stop himself anymore and followed it. He wasn't supposed to leave the yard, but he just thought the fox wanted to show him something. At first he tried to count the trees he'd passed but how could one manage such a thing inside a forest? So when the fox disappeared behind a raspberry bush and was nowhere to be found, he had no idea where he was or where home might be. He heard a river nearby and followed the sound until he found it. As he laid down to rest on its bank, no sooner had his head touched the ground than he fell into a smooth, soothing sleep.

He was woken by a delicious tinkling. It sounded like the bell his mother rang when she called him in for cake. He rubbed his eyes, stretched his hands and yawned. Then he looked around and saw that someone was sitting right next to him. A forest fairy was skipping stones on the river bank.

'Hello! I'm Daniel!'

She turned to him, smiling and fluttered her small wings.

'Aren't you going to tell me your name? Are you a fairy? You look like a fairy.'

'I am Spring. A forest fairy.'

'Can you take me home? It's almost dark and I have to go home. I'm hungry.'

'Yes, Daniel. I will take you home. Follow me!' She sat on his shoulder and pointed the way.

'Miss Spring, can we be friends? I've always wanted to meet a fairy.'

'I wish we could, Danny. But I have to leave this forest.'

'Where are you going?'

'To fairy castle. My sisters need me there to help guard the spirit of the forest.'

'Why aren't you there now?'

'Well, because one thing forest fairies do is help children who get lost in the forest find their way home. We take turns in doing it. This is my last day here. Starting tomorrow I have to return to fairy castle for the next seven years.'

'And after seven years you will come back?'

'To a forest, yes, but not here. There are many forests in the world. But a fairy will be here always. One of my sisters.'

'Can I come and see you at the castle?'

'I don't know.' she said surprised. 'No one's ever asked me that. I suppose you could. I don't think my sisters would mind.'

'So where is the castle?'

'You know where the sun sets? Somewhere over there. You just keep walking until you see a magic castle on top of a hill.'

'How will I recognize it?'

'Well, there is only one fairy castle. You will recognize it. It's covered in fairy dust.'

So all the way home, Spring told Danny about the castle and the other fairies and how the spirit of the forest was in every leaf and in every tree. Listening to her was so wonderful and her voice sounded so delicious that Danny fell in love. Simply and completely. He knew then that he would follow her wherever she went.

THE BOY WHO CHASED THE SUNSET

Almost seven years had passed, but Danny never forgot the fairy. Sometimes he made plans for the journey, but it sounded so difficult that he waited to grow up just a little more before setting off. Then one day in the schoolyard, something happened.

'Do you realize that in less than a month we're leaving school for the summer?! I can't wait! GoodBYE fifth grade!' Rosie said and something lit up in Danny's head. He'd met Spring two years before he started school, in the summer. It had been almost seven years. Seven years had passed like the wind, without bringing him any closer to her. In a couple of months she would have to leave the castle. His time was almost up.

'We have to go, Rosie! We have to go now!'

'Where?'

'I have to go somewhere. I can't tell you. I have to go now!'

'Can I come?'

'If you want to. But it's going to take a while. I don't know when we'll be coming home.'

'Ok, can I tell mom?'

'No. You either come with me now or you don't.'

'Fine! Let's get our backpacks.'
So off they went, out of the school yard, down the street with the chestnut trees that were getting ready to bloom, past the ranger's cabin, to the old road that went out of the village heading west.

119

Nobody used it anymore; the farms down that way had long closed down because of the drought. It was a beautiful road, guarded by linden trees and, strangely enough, acorn bushes grew from place to place. It seemed to just go on and on, up to the foothills of the mountains that could be seen in the horizon.

And here we are, close to where we began. The kids had been on the road the entire day. The sun was just beginning to set when they reached the corn patch.

'Danny, please! My feet hurt! I'm hungry. Let's just rest a while and gather some acorns outside the corn field. Then we can keep walking. We have to stop sometime!'

Danny turned around and paused for a moment, just enough to hear his stomach rumble.

'Ok, we can stop to eat some acorns. But then we get going; we have to cross the corn field before it gets dark.'

They went back and started picking acorns out of the big bush between the corn field and the road's end. They stuffed their pockets and then sat down in the grass, next to some stones just fit for cracking acorns.

'Well, hello there, strangers!'

'Aaaaaaaaaa!' Rosie yelled jumping to her feet. 'Who's there!'

'Who said that?' Danny grabbed a rock and jumped to his feet.

'Don't be scared. I can't move until the wind blows. I'm just an acorn tree.'

'What?'

'Push that big branch aside. Yes, the one with the little stump at the middle, that's the one. Hello again!'

'Wow! A talking acorn bush!' Rosie said.

'Hello!' Danny started. 'Why are you talking to us?'

'Well, because it's not often that I see people here. Especially children. And don't be confused, children are my favorite type of people.'

'People don't use this road anymore.'

'Indeed they don't. So why are you kids here?'

'I don't know. Why are we here, Danny? Please tell me!'

'I can't.'

'Well, I could help you if you told me,' the bush said. 'I know many things around these parts. See, me and the wind are quite good friends. He tells me everything he sees.'

'We're going to find a castle.'

'And which castle might that be, Danny?'

'A... fairy castle.'

'Oh! THE fairy castle, Danny, there is only one fairy castle.'

'What?! We're going to a fairy castle?' Rosie said surprised.

'Yes. Seven years ago I met a fairy and she's in the fairy castle now and I have to go see her before the seven years are up or I'll never see her again.'

'Marvelous choice, Danny!' the bush continued. 'I have just what you need. First of all, take the silver acorn that's hidden under my roots. I have been saving it for just such an occasion. I've always wanted to meet true adventurers and magical believers and help them on their path. It is my destiny, you see. Now, remember this. When you get to the bank of the silver river it will help you cross.'

'Thank you! Do you know where this cornfield ends? We have to cross this too and by sundown.'

'Oh, I think that'd better wait until morning, children. You look awfully tired. You can sleep under my branches and I'll speak to the wind and ask him to be warm and kind this evening.'

'I am mighty tired.' Rosie said.

'Me too. Ok, let's stop here. Thank you again, Mister. But how do you know about the silver river? Where is this river?'

'I don't know exactly, but to the west. The wind told me this years and years ago, when he brought me the acorn. But I'm sure you'll find it just like you found me. You just have to keep going.'

All being said, the children laid down in the grass. A warm wind started to blow and they immediately fell asleep.

THE BOY WHO CHASED THE SUNSET

Part III

The next day, they woke up and rubbed their eyes about seventeen times, but the acorn bush was gone. Only a silver acorn remained. Danny pocketed it and off they went through the corn field.

They walked for hours and got more and more thirsty with each step. The corn seemed to grow taller and taller and they couldn't see ahead anymore. They'd almost lost hope when, suddenly, a large shadow passed over them.

'What was that Danny?!'

'I don't know! I'm so thirsty! Maybe we're seeing things!'

'Look! Look! Aaaaaa!' Rosie yelled and ducked. Then Danny saw it. A giant white hawk was flying right above them.

'Danny! I am so scared! Oh my God, it's coming this way!'

They started to run as fast as they could but the shadow just kept getting closer and darker. Just when they thought that was the end of them...

'Stooooop!'

A powerful wind started to blow and the children tumbled round and round through the corn. When they stopped tumbling, they were sore, dizzy and dirty.

'Are you hurt? I didn't mean to do that. I'm sorry. My wings are just TOO big!'

'Danny... is the hawk talking to us? Or am I dead and seeing things?' Rosie whispered with her face covered in dirt.

'Shhh! Mr. Hawk? Are you talking to us?'

'Yes. Who else could it be?'

'You won't hurt us, will you?'

'Of course I won't. I came here to help you.'

'Help us? Help us get to the castle?'

'Yes. The wind told me you left with the silver acorn this morning but that you couldn't possibly get to the end of this corn field in time.'

'So how can you help us?'

'I will fly you out of here. Get on my back!'

The children stumbled to their feet, dusted off their shirts and pants and slowly walked towards the hawk.

'Don't be afraid. Grab on to the feathers on the back of my neck. You, my dear girl, will just have to hold on to our gentleman here. I'll go slow, don't worry. I've flown kids before.'

'Really? How?! I've only seen this in stories!' Rosie said.

'Didn't you know that most stories are true? Just because parts of the world are magic-less, doesn't mean all of it is. Now climb on!'

They did as instructed and the hawk immediately took flight. They rose above the fields and could see for miles and miles ahead. A silver line separated the yellow of the corn field from the dark green of what seemed to be a forest.

'Where are we going, Mr. Hawk?'

'See that line? That's the silver river. That's where we're going.'

'Why are you helping us, Mr. Hawk?'

'What better thing could I do? This is not a hard one to figure out. I either help someone or I don't. Time passes just the same. So I'd like to say and think that I did.'

'Thank you!'

'You're welcome, Rosie! Now hold on, we're rising above the clouds.'

'Danny... this is the most wonderful journey ever!'

THE BOY WHO CHASED THE SUNSET

As they started descending towards the river, they could make out more and more of the land below. Not just the waters were silver, like they'd imagined, but the banks as well and the trees next to it and the grass. The rocks were silver as were the bugs flying past them. As they got closer, the hawk's feather started to change color and he too became silver. They landed and when they looked at another...

'Danny... you're silver!'

'So are you Rosie!'

'Mr. Hawk, what's happening? What is this?'

'It's alright, children. The world is different here. See, for other people passing by this is just a regular river. They cross it over a bridge built downstream. In order to see that the river is silver, we ourselves have to be silver. Now I realize this may not make much sense to you now, but it will by the end of the journey.'

'What do we do now?'

'You have to get to the other side.'

'Why didn't you fly us to the other side? It's just over there!'

'The other side of the river is yet another different side of the world. I can't cross the river, only you can. I have to go now. Good luck, children! Have a safe journey!' The hawk's wings started such a rush of air when he rose towards the sky that Rosie and Danny had to hold on to one another just to stay on their feet. After they watched him fly away into the clouds, they turned to one another puzzled.

'Now what, Danny?'

'I don't know. We have to use the silver acorn, but I don't know how.'

'Maybe we're supposed to drop it into the water.'

'Maybe... or maybe crack it open.'

'How do we crack it open? It's silver!'

'Everything is silver here, isn't it? We crack a silver acorn with a silver rock.'

'Ok... you do it!'

'Fine. Bring me that boulder there.'

So Danny sat down and hit the acorn over and over again.

'It's useless. It doesn't even have a scratch on it. This can't be it.'

'Maybe we're supposed to eat it.'

'Good thinking, genius! And what if that doesn't work?'

'What if it does?'

'I don't know, but I don't think that's it. What else could we do with it?'

'Let's see. Drop it into the water, crack it, eat it... Oh, I know! We could bury it!'

'What good would that do?'

'We don't just bury it, silly, we plant it. We plant an acorn tree by burying the acorn!'

'Ok, we could try that. We can always take it out afterwards if it doesn't work. Help me dig a hole.'

The children started digging with their hands, until they had a hole about a hand's-length deep. They placed the acorn in it and covered the hole back up.

'Now what do we do?'

'Wait here!' Rosie said and headed for the river. She leaned towards the water and came back with her hands clasped around some silvery fluid, which she gently poured over the dust that covered the acorn. As soon as the last drop touched the earth, a loud crack sounded from below. Then the ground started to shake violently, like it was about to split in two.

'Look, Rosie! It's starting!'

A small silver twig came out of the earth and grew taller and taller, until it was the size of an entire tree. Then more branches started to sprout from it, swirling one around the other into a dense weave that advanced towards the river.

'It's a bridge, Rosie! We're growing ourselves a bridge! You're so smart I could hug you!'

They jumped up and down with joy, hugged screamed and laughed. When the branches touched the other river bank they were almost exhausted from all the excitement.

'We did it, Rosie! Let's cross! You can climb a tree, right?'

'Better than you can tie your shoelaces! Come on!'

They skipped from branch to branch and, soon enough, they were on the other side. But just as they touched the ground, the earth started to shake again. They held on to one another and looked as the ground swallowed back the entire bridge.

'I guess there's no way to go but forward!' Rosie said.

'Yup! Let's go!'

'Into the forest?'

'Into the forest!'

Part V

As soon as the children passed the first trees the forest closed up behind them. A row of trees appeared as if out of nowhere, so dense that the light couldn't even get through.

The forest was old and dark and there were so many leaves on the ground that they went up to your knees. Strange creaking and cracking could be heard all around.

'Danny, I'm really scared!' Rosie whispered in a mousy voice.

'Well, don't be. We got this far, didn't we? And we got all sorts of help we didn't expect. We even flew half the way. Something good is bound to happen.'

'But what if our luck ran out already?'

'Stop saying that! I didn't come all this way to stop, there's no turning back now. We are reaching that castle!'

'What castle might that be?' a loud, echoing voice said. Rosie jumped behind Danny in an instant.

'Who's there?! Show yourself!'

'Just a mere creature of the forest. I didn't mean to scare you.'

'We're not scared of anything!'

'Very well, the voice said again. I am coming to meet you then.'

The moment the creature appeared from between the trees, Danny was more afraid than he'd ever been in his entire life. He tried to stay calm, but started shaking uncontrollably. He forced himself not to run away. Behind him, Rosie's face went completely white.

The creature took a step towards them and Rosie almost fainted. Danny felt like his stomach was melting and his instincts were telling him to get as far away from there as possible. When it took another step, the children retreated a few inches and, as if it had suddenly smelled fear, the creature took out its claws and started grinning its teeth. Danny and Rosie met each other's terrified gaze. Before either of them could think, they started running for their lives.

The creature chased after them so fast Rosie could almost feel its breath on the back of her neck. They remained just ahead of the creature because they could crawl under the giant roots of the trees instead of climbing over them. They ran and the trees got thicker and thicker until they could barely see ahead anymore.

Then, the inevitable happened. Rosie tripped over Danny's leg and they crashed into the leaves, which covered them entirely. The creature sprang right after them and started digging furiously through the debris.

'Rosie, quickly! I'll tunnel through the leaves, hold on to my shirt and follow me!'

They started moving slowly but without being seen, the creature right behind them, slashing with its claws wherever it heard noise. They were heading for a hollow under the root of an old, petrified beech tree. They were only a foot away when the ground disappeared from beneath them. Danny felt like he was being sucked down a drain pipe. They were going down some sort of chute, faster and faster, like they were headed to the center of the earth. Danny felt the walls loosening, a sudden rush of cold air, and in an instant he realized that he had to swim for his life. He started moving his arms and legs and in a few moments he was drawing breath from the surface.
'Rosie! Rosie! Oh, no! Rosie!'

'I'm here, Danny! Turn around!'

'There's land behind you. Let's swim there!'

They slowly got out of the water, exhausted, scared and cold.

'What now, Danny? What do we do now?'

'I'm sorry, Rosie. I should have never taken you with me.'

'I want to be back home, safe, in front of a giant pudding. I'm terrified. How are we ever going to get out of here?'

'I think this is some sort of underground cave. There's got to be a way out if there's water here.'

'But how are going to find it?'

'I'm going to help you!'

'What?! Who said that?!'

'Don't be scared!' the tinkling voice said. 'I am a forest fairy!'

An orange speck of light appeared before them and grew brighter and brighter, until they couldn't look its way anymore.

They closed their eyes and when the light started to fade, a fairy was fluttering her wings right next to them.

'Here I am! I am Lucia. This forest's fairy. I will take you home!'

Danny's heart started to pound like thunder in a storm. In that moment he felt not that he was wet, cold, hungry and tired... But like the luckiest boy alive.

Part VI

'Wow, Danny, a real fairy!'

'Indeed I am! Look! Wings and everything! I even have a magical wand. But I don't carry it with me much, I can do magic well enough without it.'

'Lucia, my name is Danny.'

'Nice to meet you, Danny! What are two lovely children such as yourselves doing in this old, dark forest? You're the first ones I've met so far and I've been here quite a while.'

'We're going to fairy castle.'

'Pardon me, you are what?!'

'We're going to fairy castle so I can meet Spring, the forest fairy.'

'Well, that's... wonderful! I know Spring. Lovely ball of light she is. But we really have to think about how to get you to the castle. Normal people don't just stumble over it, don't you know.'

'What do you mean?'

'It's invisible to humans. Only fairies can see it.'

'But Spring told me I could come visit her.'

'Well, you can if you can find it. Let me think. There's got to be a way. Oh, by the way. Little girl, why are you going to the castle?'

'I just wanted to go with Danny. We're friends.'

'Sounds like a good enough reason. Ok, so... we could probably get you to fairy castle if we could turn you into fairies.'

'You want to turn me into a fairy?'

'Do you have boy fairies?'

'We sure do. Us girls would get mighty lonely without them.'

'I'd love to be a fairy!' Rosie said. 'Can you make that happen?'

'Well... no. We have to visit our fairy godmother and she has to agree. Far as I know, she decides who does or does not enter the realm of fairies. We're going to go meet her right now. Sit tight, I'm just going to sprinkle this fairy dust all over you and off we'll go.'

Danny and Rosie held on to one another as Lucia put some fairy dust in her palm and blew it over the tops of their heads. No sooner had she done so as bright sparks appeared everywhere. They grew bigger and bigger and started to swirl around clockwise, like a whirlwind. They both felt dizzy and didn't even realize they couldn't feel their feet on the ground anymore. Then, just as they had appeared, the lights vanished and they woke up next to a little shack, on top of a hill. The sun was getting ready to set and the sky was pink and violet and the fields of wheat they could see in the distance seemed to wave slowly in the light wind. It was a warm summer evening, their clothes felt clean and soft again and they could smell the delicious scent of cherry pie drifting from the window of the shack.

'Go on, knock!' Lucia said, but her voice was different. It didn't sound as much like a bell anymore, but rather like a sweet and nonetheless normal girl's voice. Danny and Rosie both turned around. Instead of a fairy, they now saw a girl their age, with curly hair in two ponytails, large front teeth and big blue eyes.

'Don't be so surprised. This is my human figure. We have to meet godmother this way so you two can see and talk to her. Now go on, knock.'

Danny gently tapped the door with his knuckles. The door immediately opened.

'Go on in then!'

They pushed the door open a little bit further, to reveal the loveliest little cabin they'd ever seen. Everything looked small and cozy as could be. The windows had colorful curtains held up with rows of ribbons. The furniture seemed to be made entirely out of white birch, engraved with flowers, butterflies, trees and stars. Next to a little stove in the corner, pots and pans hanged on the walls. They were hand painted with flowers, ladybugs and clouds. On the table stood a large vase filled with fresh flowers and wheat ears that gave off a beautiful smell. And on each of the four plates on the table there was a big piece of cherry pie.

'This is wonderful!' Rosie said. 'And I am so hungry! Do you think the pie is for us?!'

'I'm sure it is. Let's sit down. Godmother! We've arrived! Please come to greet us.'
'Lucia!' a woman's voice sounded from outside. 'Keep the children company, please. I'll be right with you. I'm getting fresh water from the stream.' In a moment the door opened again and a beautiful young woman came in. She had a white dress on, painted with small pink roses, and a pink apron over it, with two large pockets. Her hair was held neatly in a bun, her cheeks were red and she had a big smile on her face.

'Here you are! I've been waiting for you for three days! Have some pie, you must be starving! Come on, don't be shy.'

The children each grabbed their piece of pie and started eating heartily, without taking their eyes off the young woman.

'I know you want to reach fairy castle. I was expecting you. But before we go there, I have to tell you why you got this far. No human has ever seen fairy castle. It is a precious place and we guard it, because inside it we keep the spirit of the forest. Before you, no one has ever even asked us about the castle. Our sisters took lost children home, but as soon as they arrived, the children forgot all about them. That's why the world never found out that fairies truly exist. Then you met Spring and fell in love and this love preserved the memory in your heart. This, for us, is of great importance. It is the moment your world meets ours for the first time. So you, not just you Danny, but both of you children, have a task ahead. You will see fairy castle but you have to tell the world that fairies exist and that they protect not only children who are lost in the woods but also the spirit of the forest.'

'How can we do that? Who will believe us?' Rosie asked.

'Other children will believe you, Rosie. And they will believe in magic and the world will be a little bit better of a place.'
'Ok, Miss Godmother. We will tell other children about the castle. Can we please go there now? Spring is about to leave to another forest and I have to see her. I just have to.'

'Very well, Danny. Let's go outside now.'

They went outside and the sunset had taken over the entire sky leaving them feeling as though they were standing under an orange dome. Shards of yellow splashed in all directions, like gold was running down in streams to the world's edges. Danny suddenly remembered Spring's words. The castle was on top of a hill where the sunset. It was covered in fairy dust. He turned around and looked at the cottage again, but he could only see an eruption of light that shot up from the top of the hill, into the sky. Golden dust started to rain around them and he realized...

'We're there, Rosie!'

'We're there, Danny!' Rosie also yelled and they hugged and started jumping up and down with glee.

The light slowly dimmed and the castle started to take shape. It had dozens of little towers and balconies that buzzed with the tinkling voices of fairies. Danny looked around hoping to discover Spring when...

'Danny! You found me!'

'Spring! You're still here! I'm so glad you're still here! Oh! What's happening?! Spring!'

Danny felt like he was being pulled down by an invisible force. Then he turned to Rosie and understood.

'Rosie! We're shrinking!'

'I know! And look! You have wings on your back!'

'So do you!'

'We're turning into fairies!'

'Don't worry, Spring said. You're almost ready. There! There you are. Now start flapping your wings. Look at me. Great! You can do it! Wonderful! Now... follow me!'

So off they flew into the castle, and here starts the epilogue of our story. They lived happily in the castle until they learned everything there was to know about the world of the fairies. Then the day came to keep their promise so, hand in hand, the three of them, Danny, Rosie and Spring, started their journey home.

The hawk flew them from the castle all the way back to the old road where they'd started. When they got home is was as if no time had passed at all. They went back to living the life of regular kids and the years slowly passed them by. But they never forgot their promise, and when they grew up, Danny became a writer of fairy tales. Rosie illustrated his books with drawings, and Spring opened a bookstore where children could come after school to hear stories of the fairy castle. All in all, the world was a little bit better and they all lived happily ever after.

THE UNUSUAL ADVENTURE OF THE WILD CHICKEN

Part I

One day, Christy the wild chicken decided to build a bridge on top of the only hill in Breezy Plains: the one at the eastern border, where the fox held his acclaimed speeches on freedom and democracy.

She started gathering twigs, branches, leaves of grass and wheat and piled them up neatly, at the side of the hill. Then she carried them to the top one by one. Hundreds of times she went up and down the hill, until almost every little thing had been moved.

As she struggled with the last of the pumpkin leaves, the forest rustled in the distance. Christy looked up and saw the wave traveling above the fields of wheat. A cold forest wind was coming her way. She sat down to rest as the wind threw her entire day's work into the air, spun it around and scattered it all across the field below.

Most spotted chickens would have given up then. But not Christy. She whizzed across the field again and piled everything back up in no time. Then, she fell asleep with her head tucked safely under a rose branch, right next to the assortment of half-dried things she had worked so dearly to collect.

The next morning she was on her feet before sunrise. Filled with liveliness and momentum, she ran each and every twig, leaf or piece of bark right up the hill again. About four hours later, just as the sun was getting almost impolitely hot, she was carrying one of the last birch twigs when she heard the forest rustle again. The wind came in a single, uncaring spiral, that whooshed everything up into the air and spread it all across the field for the second time.

'Well, this is odd! There must be some sort of enchantment on this hill! Hmm... I'll just go see the witch of Breezy Plains and she'll help me see to it. What a lovely place this would be for a bridge!'

She set off immediately and was knocking on the witch's door faster than you could recite the alphabet backwards.

'Who dares to interrupt my beauty sleep?' sounded a coarse, and surprisingly young voice.

'It's me, Christy! I come seeking advice about the hill. I think there's an enchantment on it.'

'Fine, step inside. The door is open. And please pet my fish. Or I shall not give you counsel.'

Christy stuck the tip of her feathers inside the round, transparent fishbowl by the door and gently stroked Albus, the witch's albino goldfish.

'Good! I sense Albus likes you! Come in, then. I'm in the kitchen.'

'Weren't you sleeping?' Christy called, while untying her chicken shoes.

'No, that's just a phrase I use to amuse myself. Now please, sit down and tell me about this hill.'

Christy told the story of how the time and materials she had put into building a bridge had been blown away by the wind twice, without any excuse or warning. As she finished her last sentence, the witch pulled out an enormous old book from right under the table they were sitting at.

'Let's see!' she said. 'Local enchantments, page 1457. Here we are! Yes! There are three enchantments on that hill. You must remove them all to build anything. I am going to tell you what to do and you have to listen to me carefully. You may not write anything down. Are you ready, wild chicken?'

'I am.'

THE UNUSUAL ADVENTURE OF THE WILD CHICKEN

Part II

'Now listen here! First of all, there is a charm on that hill, set there by its builder.'

'Its builder?!'

'Do not interrupt me, please, I am still talking! Now... yes, by its builder. That hill wasn't always there, which makes a lot of sense really, given that it is the only hill around. A giant mole built it. He was the largest of all moles and accidentally destroyed the mole king's castle when he sneezed. That's why he was cast away, never to return underground. But moles can't live in the open air, so the scheme he came up with was to just build himself a hill. That way he could be above ground and under it at the same time. Pretty smart, no?'

'Quite!'

'Then, the mole, infuriated by the banishment, placed a charm on the hill. No one can build anything over it or under it. He wanted his home to be left to himself and himself alone. There you have it!'

'So what do I do?'

'Well, you get the mole to remove the charm.'

'But how do I find him?'

'Well, you can't. He's dead. Like really, really dead. He died a looooong time ago.'
'Splendid! So do I have to dig him out or something? Invoke his spirit? What?'

'No, nothing of the sort, you silly hen. What bad movies have you been watching?! My lord, no! I know his great-great-great-grandson! Morose Mole! He lives just a few bushes away from me, in that direction. He's a stubborn, bitter character. He wouldn't help a soul if his lunch depended on it! He can remove the charm if he sees fit. He just has to climb on top of the hill, roll over twice, clap his paws five times, spiral his tail, touch his nose and say: Hilltop of my family tree / You are now forever free!'

'Very well then. I will go persuade Mr. Mole to undo the spell. Can I please come back afterwards?'

'Certainly. This is quite fun. I'm very curious as to how you'll manage to convince that old spoilsport. He's more off his rocker than I am. Now shoo! I have to go play a waltz for my geese. They hate it when I ruin their classical music evening.'

Christy scooted right on over to the mole's house. He lived in a dark hollow, hidden by a thick layer of fern. Approaching his door, she quickly put on a bowler hat and navy blue necktie she carried around for just such occasions. She then buttoned her coat and officially knocked. After quite some time, a series of slouchy footsteps were heard and a bored-looking mole, quite past its first youth, answered sourly.

'What do you want?'

'Excuse me, is this the residence of Morose Mole?'

'Yes. I am he. What do you want?'

'I am from the Breezy Plains Department of Forestry Property and Administration. I have come to inform you that your inheritance has cleared.'

'Oh, what are you blabbering on about?'

'Your great-great-great-grandfather, the titan mole, built a hill just outside this grove that is now being passed on to you. You just have to come and take it into custody.'

'Fine. I'll come if you just leave me alone. What do I have to do?'

'I will tell you precisely what when we get there. It's just a small ceremony. Please come with me!'

The mole went with Christy and, without further ado, he said the words and the first charm was dispelled. Then back to the witch's house it was, for the second challenge.

THE UNUSUAL ADVENTURE OF THE WILD CHICKEN

'Well that was quick!' the witch couldn't help but remark when Christy showed up at her door again. 'Did you get the old grouch to undo the charm?'

'Indeed I did! That hill would be a lovely place for a bridge.'

'You want to build a bridge on top of the hill? Is that what you want to do with your twigs?'

'Yes.'

'A bridge to what?'

'Just over the hill. It's a lovely place for a bridge. Just to cross from one side to the other.'

'But that makes no sense whatsoever! It's like sewing a sewing machine or pouring some water into the ocean, or what have you.'

'There's no harm in that though, is there?'

'I suppose there isn't. But why do you want to do it if it's absolutely pointless?'

'Oh, I think it'll be beautiful. I imagine that when the sun sets people will watch it from the bridge. And they will see the world below like through a window. And you always see things better through a window. You never notice how beautiful something is until you've stared at it from out of a window.'

'So you want to build a bridge that'd be like a window to see the world through.'

'Yes!'

'And why have it on top of the hill? For the view I presume?'

'That as well. No particular reason. Just seems like a better place than others. A bridge in the middle of a field would just look plain ridiculous, don't you think?'

'I suppose it would. Now... to continue as I do not have all day, the second charm! It says in my book that once upon a time, a seagull stopped to rest on this hill on his way to the seashore. He liked it so much that he decided to return here one day. But in order for him to find the hill, it had to remain unchanged. So there you have it. He put a spell on the hill so that no one would change its appearance.'

'Well, how do I undo this one?'

'I don't know. See, I don't do bird charms. I'm good with rodents, mammals and fish, but not birds. Don't know why exactly, just didn't much enjoy the practice in witchcraft school. You can't learn everything either. Anyway, it's not my specialty. So I don't know. You'll have to find out for yourself.'

'Fine. I'll find the seagull then. Do you know where he is?'

'By the northern seashore, I presume. Many miles that way!'

Now Christy was, for one of the first times in her breezy life, perplexed. What to do? The trip could take ages and be the death of her. What oh what was to come of this? Surely someone must be going that way. Someone faster than her, someone who could deliver a message. But who? Who did she know that traveled north often? Who had giant wings and the agility of an eagle? Who?! Except... the eagle!

Christy rushed to the eagle's tree and started pecking on the bark. It took hours for the eagle to show himself. As he flew down to stop the annoying pecking, he had very little patience left for discussions or favors.

'Mr. Eagle, Sir, please don't be mad. I have something to kindly ask of you. Do you, by any chance, know a seagull that travels around these parts?'

'I do. Sea Lion, the seagull. The bravest, most honest seagull in the whole world. What's it to you?'

'Oh, I am in luck today! Sir, I need to send him a message. A very, very important message.'

'And how does that concern me?'

'Sir, I am but a poor hen and would take me ages to deliver it. But if you should meet him in the near future, it would help me greatly if you delivered this message for me.'

'Fine. I don't like you in particular, but as long as I can easily remember the message, I'll deliver it.'

'Could you please ask him to come back to the hill he loves? I want to build something there and he put a spell over it.'

'So you want to ruin his beloved hill and me to help?'

'No, I'll only make it better. Please, I don't ask for much. Just tell him for me that a wild chicken wants to build something wonderful atop his beautiful hill.'

'Fine. I tell him you want to build something and I think he'll come. He's a good bird, he is.'

'Thank you, Mr. Eagle, Sir! Thank you! I am forever indebted.'

'I fly north with some errands the day after tomorrow. When I come back in the evening visit me about his response. Have a good day and please let me be.'

'Thank you! I most certainly will!'

THE UNUSUAL ADVENTURE OF THE WILD CHICKEN

Part IV

When the three days had passed, the wild chicken was back pecking away at the eagle's tree again. For hours she pecked but nothing happened. So she pecked way into the night and only when she was so tired that she could hardly move her head, she went home to sleep. But the next morning there she was again, chipping the bark with her pointy beak. Again, though, nothing happened. And this went on for a week or so, every day Christy pecked at the tree relentlessly. Until, one night...

'Who, in the name of all that is green, dares to wake me?'

'Sir... Sir, it is me. The wild chicken. You have a message for me sir?'

'Oh, it's the crazy hen is it? Shoo, you goofy, obnoxious animal! You pest you! Leave me be!'

'Sir, you have a message for me. Until you tell me what it is, I will not let you be.'

Infuriated, the eagle shot down towards Christy, all menacing, with his night cap still on and slippers on his feet. He pinned her to the tree with his mighty wings and as she struggled to free herself, he hissed:

'When I say leave me be you...'

He stopped in mid-sentence as the wind blew away his pink night hat.

'Oh, no!' And away he turned and made for the pink garment that was swooped right beneath the root of a tree. He clawed and pecked and flapped his wings as hard as he could but he could not get it to move. So, alas, he had to admit defeat and finally say:

'Wild chicken... would you please retrieve my headdress for me? I am in dire need of it.'

'Certainly sir. My message, please?' Christy said, without pride or contempt.

'He said you can build anything you want. He found a new summer home in the north. He has already undone the charm.'

'Splendid! Here you go, then!'

'The eagle gently hugged the pink piece of fabric, smelled it and flew back atop his tree without another word.

'How strange the world is,' Christy thought. 'And they call me crazy for wanting to build a bridge. What about the animals that don't build anything?' She slowly made her way home, pondering the eagle's affection for his hat. 'Such a strong creature... such a weak heart!' She fell asleep remembering her own parents. Two moderately average hens of no particular qualities or means that had raised her in no specific way. The next day she was banging on the witch's door again.

'Come in, dear! I want you to meet my pet snake! This is Helena! Once upon a time she ate your grandmother. Bony chicken she was, apparently. Now, listen here!'

'Excuse me? Which one of my grandmothers?!'

'The old one.'

'Which one of the old ones?'

'The one with the red nail polish on her beak.'

'Oh, her. Oh, that's alright, I never really liked her much.'

'Very well, then. Now, this grandmother of yours carried around the magical key to a magical chest.'

'So?'

'So in the chest there is a small plank of wood. A magical plank of wood that floats!'

'Most wood floats.'

'Fine, miss smarty pants. I see you don't need my advice, then. Go undo the third charm yourself.'

'I'm sorry! Do carry on!'

'So this magical plank of wood can talk, you see. And it is the only remaining plank from the castle that used to be on top of the hill. It was destroyed ages ago by a giant rabbit. If you want to build anything on top of that hill, you will have to start with that plank. It has to become part of your bridge.'

'So where do I find the key that your snake ate and the chest?'

'I have the chest. And I know where Helena has been going about her business for years. Here's a small shovel. I will show you the way.'

THE UNUSUAL ADVENTURE OF THE WILD CHICKEN

Part V

Yet again, without pride or remorse, Christy was working towards building her bridge. For two whole days she dug around the snake compost heap that the witch had indicated. Suddenly, out of nowhere on the third day...

'It's alright, dear, you can stop now' the witch said.

'Why? I haven't found the key yet. If it's here I'll find it.'

'But it's not there.'

'Well how do you know that? You're the one that told me where to look, in the first place.'

'Precisely. I only wanted you to dig up the heap so I wouldn't have to do it. I need that compost for my fig trees, you see. I grow them behind the house next to my cactuses.'

'So all my work for the past two days is absolutely pointless?'

'But of course not! It made me merry as can be. So now I can tell you where the key really is. You proved you deserve it.'

'Because I dug up this heap?'

'Honey, anyone willing to scoop snake poop just to fulfill a dream is sure going to fulfill it eventually. By now, you shouldn't even need my help. You just don't know that. You'd find a way no matter what.'

'I suppose I would. That would be such a lovely place for a bridge.'

'Now think about it. Where is this key?'

'Did your snake actually eat my grandmother?'

'Yes.'

'Well, then, if it's not here, it should be around your house somewhere. Except you knew you were coming to see me. So you probably have it with you right now.'

'You're pretty smart for a hen, you are. Here it is. This is the key' the witch said and handed over something like a rusty screw.

'What about the chest, then?'

'Come inside. Let's open it up.'

Right under Albus' fish tank, there was a bulky, dusty old box, shaped like a pear. The witch moved the fish and Christy looked for a keyhole. Sure enough, she found something resembling one and inserted the key. The screw started to move by itself, twitching and squirming like a worm. It then opened a pair of small beady eyes and said:

'Oh, bother! How I missed my home! Who has brought me back?! Is it you?'

'It's me. Can you look around your house for something like a stick or a plank, please?'

'Certainly. I know what you mean. I met a hen once and she left me with a small piece of wood. But it's not a plank, really, it's very small. She said you should bury it.'

'That will do. Thank you.'

The screw-worm brought out a tiny piece of wood out of his pear and Christy happily went along and dug a hole in the ground on the side of the hill. That's where she started building a majestically simple wooden bridge. The wind blew things away no more and she was almost done in a fortnight. Afterwards, she went to see the world from her bridge almost every single morning. Usually by herself, until one happy day, a badger was also out and about, staring into the distance. The next day, so was a small penguin. The third day, a giraffe stretched to see the horizon. And by the end of the summer just about every species of animal you can imagine took its turn at looking at the world in a new way.

'I am happy,' Christy thought. 'This is a lovely place for a bridge.'

THE LIFE OF THE ELEMENTS

THE MAGICAL MELODY FROM THE VILLAGE OF TREES

Part I

Once upon a time there was a village of trees, at the foothills of a tall, grey mountain. It never rained on the mountain and nothing ever grew upon it. But it was said that beneath it ran a stream of the world's purest water. That this stream kept the entire world at its foothills alive, made from rain and snow and rivers and oceans and even the icebergs of Antarctica. But there was no proof or recollection or any knowledge, in any form, to prove that such a thing were possible.

The trees had settled in the village many generations before with the great forest migration that ended the dark ages. Their forefathers had lived on the mountain when it was green and life burst from every crease and crevasse. But one day, the sky darkened above it and the crest of the mountain remained dark for the days to come. And all the stirring and sounding on it slowly died away as the ground became as barren as the sky and the animals started to move away.

One day, at the council of the forest elders, it was decided that each and every tree would uproot itself, and together they would search for a new land to call home. They dragged their roots across the stony paths so slowly that nothing was ever visible to mortal eyes. But yet they walked ceaselessly, for eras and eras, until the gentle, thin, mossy bark of their feet first touched upon green grass again. They finally settled at the foothills of the mountain, and the procession of putting the forest in order again lasted for many human years, more than anyone would care to count.

Then, one evening as the sun was setting by the mountain, behind a hapless storm cloud that lay too far away to seem threatening to anyone in the wood, a single leaf fell from the tallest branch of the oldest beech tree. On its way down, it gently nudged the driest of the twigs, which snapped out of place and fell to the floor of the wood. Down it went, sliding along roots and wet leaves, all the way to the ground that welcomed it as the last piece in dire need of coming into place. The great migration was complete and the long life of the village started.

It is after this moment that the trees started knitting their branches into rooftops. With each passing year they pressed them closer and closer together, until, from above, the forest looked like a forgotten medieval castle, with high, pointed arches and ribbed vaults.

When the work was almost complete a faint and strange sound started to make its way through the heavy, time worn trunks. It was as if the wind was blowing through the leaves, or, perhaps, as if someone was playing an old, rusty harp. At first only a mere alternation of faded high notes sounded. But it grew, slowly and gently, until it became a melody that vaguely vibrated with the breath of the entire forest. That moment, that simple suspended instant when the sounds became music, eventually changed everything.

THE MAGICAL MELODY FROM THE VILLAGE OF TREES

Part II

The melody changed with the passing of each day and night. It grew with the forest, from it and around it, as if it were the sound of living itself.

It seemed to be constantly adding instruments. At first, there was just the harp. Then came the flute, right before the first violin. And following that violin came countless others, in numerous voices and tones, like different species of birds all singing together. An orchestra was coming into being with the grace and discretion of the morning breeze.

The depth of the song heightened and all the noise and clutter was peeled from it as it learned the ways of being above ground. But through the ages, no one had yet listened to it or cared for it or understood it in a way not sewn into the fabric of nature. Until that fateful day, when a speck appeared on the horizon, soon to become a line, and eventually a vaguely outlined silhouette. Of a man. In old age.

He slowly walked towards the forest. It seemed it would take him an eternity to arrive from the end of the horizon to the tall village of green roofs and grey bark. His back was slightly hunched, but his steps were firm, and in his right hand he carried a tall wooden staff, engraved with leaves and birds and flames. For just a moment, when the light of the sun fell upon the contour of a flame, the wind stopped and the light froze and ripples erupted all around him. They hit the village walls and the forest elders, shaking their arms and leaves and knees, understood that the visitor held both their life and death in his hands.

He could smell the still alarm he had started in the dew of the morning and he knew from the rattling of the leaves that the forest held council. He proceeded to advance with measured steps. Had anyone been there to bear witness, they might have seen that the soles of his feet left no footprints on the grass, for where he stepped the blades appeared as if never touched.

As he drew nearer, the rattling faded and the village of trees remained completely still. The spirits of the forest were silent, waiting to find some sign of his intentions. He made his way to the foothills of the mountain, in between the rocky slope and the village, and there he turned his back to the forest and stared at the dark tip of the mountain.

He raised both his hands above his head, with his staff in his right, and in an instant he delivered a blow that echoed throughout the forest. The sound leapt through the trees, eating away at the silence from every hollow and crack. The mountain quivered with the strength of the stroke and it
seemed like the world itself was shaking. So the leaves began to rustle.

Their rustling grew louder and stronger than the sound of the hit, and under the arched rooftop of the forest it climbed. As the sun rose over the edge of the trees and shone through it, it turned into the loudest melody the forest had ever played. It erupted through the roof and trees and swept everything in its path, heading towards the place where the mountain had taken the blow.

THE MAGICAL MELODY FROM THE VILLAGE OF TREES

Part III

As the melody flooded each and every grain of space, the mountain started to vibrate. Cliffs renounced their stillness and trembled as if frozen to the bone. With thundering crashes, enormous shards of rock tumbled down the lifeless walls and smashed into the dark canyons that laid untouched for ages. The entire mountain seemed to be falling apart bit by bit. Out of the clouds surrounding its peak, giant spear shaped boulders continued to rain down on the plateaus below.

The old man stood watching, with the gnarled staff in his right hand barely touching the lower leaves of an oak. As the blades brushed past the coarse, dry wood, thin threads of white light rose from its veins and crept up the thin branch to the almost rotten trunk that barely held life enough to save its own leaves until the fall. The tree was dying. But the light slowly tiptoed through every crack, like a pure and shallow river that ran upwards, and where it touched the bark and the crumbled vessels the cells of the wood healed and came together, and the whole of the body of the tree was slowly returning to being, new and alive once more.

He didn't even care to notice what good he was doing as he modestly stood staring at the ravished mountain. The song of the forest grew louder and louder, until the tremor turned into a powerful earthquake, causing the ground of the desolate mountain and the village of trees above it to shake and shiver and pulsate with anguish. Everything appeared to be preparing for an imminent end, while barely a hair off his white head had moved in the midst of all the rattling of the world.

And with the simple, resounding crack of a whip, just before everything was ready to collapse, the mountain split in two and a mile-wide stream of clear water shot up to the sky, eager and hungry to escape the bowels of the earth that had been keeping it trapped for so long.

Upon reaching the sky, it pierced the veil of clouds and millions of rays and reflections fell with it back to the ground, as the first inhabitants of a new era. But no one could have foreseen that the thirst of the song would be quenched as the rain of water and light fell down upon the earth, and that the music would start to quiet down with the quake.

The old man raised a hand to his forehead. The shadow of the staff cast a dark stripe on his old, grey clothes. He turned around and as slowly as he had arrived, he paced back towards the line of the horizon, while every leaf of grass remained untouched behind him.

THE MOUNTAIN THAT BUILT A WORLD

'Mmm... morning again! Wow, how blue the sky is today. The clouds are tickling my back more than usual, too. Feels like a good day. Maybe today is the day.

'Sky! Can you hear me up there? Hello? Sky? Come on, I know you're out there! You've got to be out there just like I am here. Don't pretend you can't hear me, I know you must hear something. Sky! Please answer! Please! I'm really grateful for you sending the clouds my way every morning. I don't especially like it when they rain on my toes, but their general fluffiness makes me feel better. Sky! Please say something! I'm so... alone. Sheesh...

'Well, maybe today is not the day. What day is it anyway? I don't know. How long has it been since I've last seen anybody? I know I saw a bird a few million years ago. Strange creature she was... looked more like a dolphin with wings to me. I can't even remember what year I'm in. 153 million plus something extra. I wonder if that's a lot in bird years. Probably depends on the bird.

'I wish I could meet somebody new. I'd love having someone to talk to. Maybe one day the sky will answer. Or the sun. I'm going to try him again tomorrow. What if I'm just obnoxious and they don't want to talk to me? But how would they know? By talking to other mountains? So there'd be other mountains in the world. I think I should see them, though. I am pretty tall, after all.

'Oh, how lonely I feel. I wish I had a friend. Just any friend. I would take care of my friend and we could spend time together. All the time. I wonder if time passes differently when you're with someone. Could it? Where does time go when it passes, anyway? Where are those 152 million years that were once here? Do they go around the world so that other beings can have time? Or do they just disappear? Is time present everywhere at once or just in certain places? If it passes differently when you're with someone then it should not be the same time all around. I'm confused, though. I have no idea how I know about time anyway. Seems like a strange thing to know about. Just like friends.

'How do I know I'm supposed to have a friend? Have I ever had a friend? Maybe I did. Maybe Sky and I were once friends. Made of the same stuff. The sky and I and the sun and his little sister. Sounds like a fun gang.

'Oh, the sun's setting already. That's a lovely shade of red, right There. I should grow something green to go with that red. I could get like a soft, green cover. Yes, that's just what I'm going to do!

'But how? I could sprout it! I think that once, when I was little I sprouted this little poofy green thing, like a ball of twigs covered in layers of green scales. I will definitely try that again!'

So the mountain tried and tried but he could not sprout a tree. 'Hmm... maybe I'm missing something. I remember that back then the water from the clouds all dripped into one place, like a terribly long wave.

'Clouds! Clouds! Please come here! I need some rain for my toes, please. Could you please all concentrate on wetting the same spot? Thank you! That brown one over there is good. Seems to be softer than all the gray parts. Oh, that actually
feels good. Now here goes!'

So the mountain tried to make something grow again and with the soil moist enough, grass appeared in no time.

'How lovely! A bit lighter than the shade I was looking for, but it's a start. Now how do I grow that? I need more earth, seems it won't grow on rock.

'Oh, I know! This is going to be fun!'

THE MOUNTAIN THAT BUILT A WORLD

'Oh, it's night already! No matter, the sun will just set again tomorrow. I might as well get everything ready until then. More ground is what I need. So here goes it!'

The mountain started to shake and shake and at first nothing seemed to happen. Until a giant cliff started swaying threateningly above a crevasse, scratching the clouds above with its tip. In moments, the white clouds angered and turned into a storm. They started shooting lightning bolts at the mountain and called on a strong wind that swept everything in its path to bring down the cliff. The wind blew with such force that it took down the wobbling peak in a mere instant.

The enormous piece of rock crashed and started a domino of falling cliffs, which smashed into the crevasse, one over the other, with thundering sounds, until the whole side of the mountain was bare. The crevasse was topped with rock and the clouds, happy to be left unscratched, ended the rain and brought back the stars.

'That went well!' the mountain thought. 'Alas, it is only the first step. I still have some ground to make come about. That should be a bit easier. I know I've got a lot of it.... how do I make it come out, though? I wish I had me some paws. I'd be done already if I did. Creatures with paws dreadfully underestimate their possibilities. Now, let's see. I think that if I concentrate hard enough, I could just do what I think I can. Shouldn't be too difficult. Mud flying up in the air, then falling back and covering most of the rock in one thick layer of soil. An earth volcano! That's what I'm going to be!'

So the mountain concentrated and concentrated until, after three days, a bubbling noise was heard from underneath a canyon.

169

'Splendid! Finally! I'm so glad I didn't give up after the first day! I missed four sunsets already but how gorgeous are the remaining ones going to be! Now just a little more effort and...'

The canyon's bottom cracked and hot mud started flying into the air. The clouds thought it was raining tar, so they got out of the way and frowned at the silly mountain. Everything was now brown and murky. 'Gorgeous! This is the liveliest I've ever been! So close I am to being green, I can't wait! Oh, the clouds have gone away. Well, no matter, they'll be back soon when they see how good I look in my new green cover. I wonder why I didn't just start doing this before. It's so much fun. Why has the thought never occurred to me? I've been looking at beautiful sunsets for ages now. Maybe... sometimes you just have to grow into things.

Maybe I just grew into becoming green. That's a bit of a scary thought, though. No, that can't be right. Had I known I could do this, I would have definitely done it earlier. I'm never going to just wait on things to happen like I did before. I think there is a new age, over me. One where I can be, instead of see, when I can make instead of take. That sounds mighty philosophical, doesn't it? I wish I had someone to tell it to.

'Sky... are you out there?! Please answer me, Sky!'

THE MOUNTAIN THAT BUILT A WORLD

'You know, I wish I had your eyes, Sky. Blue and soft and high above everything. I wish you told me about the world. I wish I understood where the beautiful sunsets come from. How small I am. Tall as a mountain, but so tiny compared to the sky. But I am still going to finish what I started. I have plenty of earth now and it has rained all night, and it is time for me to sprout a green cover.'

The mountain thought green as hard as he could and soon enough he started feeling something fuzzy tickling his toes.

'Oh, it's started! I will make a mess of green out! And Sky will look at me and know, regardless if she admits or says it, that in this still and changeless world, I made something!'

The grass spread across the mountain and covered all the earth it could find. Then, berry bushes started to appear, at first barely enough of them to feed a baby bird. But more of them grew and grew, until there were no more bushes but berry patches that covered the plateaus and slopes. The mountain opened its eyes, as if awoken from a deep sleep.

'Red! I made red! And blue and violet! I made all these things! And how fragile they are! How small and feeble they seem with their short, innocent spikes. Just like I may as well be compared to the sky. I had no idea I could do this! What are these beings? Are they animals? Am I just seeing things? Is the sunset just reflecting back into my skin? I am confused. Sky! You must have seen them before. What are they?'

But the sky didn't answer so the mountain fell asleep wondering. The next day he opened his eyes slowly, as if he was afraid to see what lay before them. What if everything had only been a dream?

He could feel a wave of joy growing inside him at the memory of the colors he'd created.

'If I made this, there might be so many other things I could bring to life! Plants that grow until they touch the sky, flowers that cover everything around them in petals, fruit that sweetens the ground it falls on and maybe even... Animals! And I wouldn't have to be alone anymore. Ever.

'But where do I start? Where on earth do I start?! I could just make a bigger plant. See how that works out. Yes! Now...'

So the mountain concentrated on bringing about something like a tree and, indeed, one quickly came about. A white birch tree. Tall and slender, like all birch trees.

'How gracious this creature is for its height. I must make more of its sort!' And by the end of the day, the sunset reflected into a white and green field of trees.

'I feel I've done something good today. This is probably the most beautiful arrangement of colors I have ever seen. Sky! I know you're not going to answer me but I'm sure you feel a little proud. Your clouds aren't alone anymore. They can rain over someone just as white. Now... it's already late. And I have so many things to make tomorrow! I'll be off to sleep now, Sky. Maybe you could say a word to me in the morning. If only one...'

THE MOUNTAIN THAT BUILT A WORLD

Part IV

'Sky, I've had my green cover for years now. I've grown flowers and bushes and trees in every color I could imagine. They have leaves or blades or not even, and they either enjoy the sunlight or they don't, and they either drink plenty of water or they don't. And there is so much life running through the green veins of everything I've made! I can hear it buzzing as it flows from each and every one of these creatures into all the others.

But how to transform this into a friend, I still don't know. But I am not giving up either. You know that millions of years ago we both saw a dolphin with wings. I didn't know where it came from then or where it went or why there was only one that made it this far. Now that everything is green, I will make that happen again. I will have animals roaming these places. So I've been trying to remember how I've come to know about these creatures. Why I knew about birds and dolphins and not about plants.

'The only thing I could find, deep inside my memory, is that there used to be animals here before me. When I was a baby, just a stump in the ground. I wasn't always this big. Once I was just about the size of a tree. I could actually see mountains in the distance and envy them because they were so close to you, Sky. I thought surely you must be friends. Then one day I heard a loud thundering in the bowels of the earth. And it seemed for a while like the whole world was going to crumble.

The ground cracked so deeply I remember I could see the molten rock in the deep gushing towards the surface. That's when I started to grow. Something pushed me from underneath, higher and higher until I found myself way above the clouds. I started calling out for my friends but there was no one else there. Just me with my cliffs and crevasses and you, Sky. So I was happy for a little while and forgot that I was never supposed to be there.

173

'Now I remember that I am not, in fact, a mountain. Just a lucky stump. And I used to have friends and animals roaming all around me and I'm going to make that happen again. I am going to call upon the strongest of the winds to bring me flocks of birds and I will take care of them. And then they will tell the other animals what a paradise they've found here and the others will come, and I will hear voices again and my forests will be filled with families and friends and stories.

'But I need your help to do that, Sky. I can't call the wind by myself. He is your friend, he never took that much of a liking to me. I think he sees me as more of an obstacle. Speak to the wind, Sky, please. I will ask you every day until you do.'

Thus the mountain spoke, and afterwards he waited. Days passed and every one of them he would renew his pleading to the sky. Yet nothing happened. For years this went on and the mountain never lost hope. Every morning he would wake up and think that this might be the day, the best of days.

Then, one night, when the mountain was fast asleep, the leaves of the birch trees started rustling. A gentle breeze made its way through the branches. The clouds gathered above into a circle, around the moon, as it shone its light on the tip of the sleeping mountain. And then, as if the whole world had plotted for everything to fall magically into place, a warm wind started to blow, right from the sky, down unto the mountain. And animals began to rain down from between the clouds, by the dozens. Frogs, birds, foxes and wolves, bears and deer, all fast asleep and gently carried down with the force of the wind.

Before the first rays of sunlight had pierced the clouds over the horizon, the mountain's forests were filled with life that was just waiting to open its eyes and be in all the wondrous ways of being.

Sky, however, never answered. And if she heard him or the storm was just a coincidence, we will never truly know. Our beliefs, however, are free to be what they may.

174

THE BOAT BUILDER FROM THE MOUNTAIN VILLAGE

Part I

'I am building a boat,' Arthur slowly said. 'I will sail it across this mountain. Until I am on the other side of it and here no more.'

'Nonsense!' said a stranger. 'Crazy old man!' he muttered as he wandered away on the winding streets of the village.

Arthur spoke in a soft, crooked voice that always seemed to ponder every word. He had been a good father and an even better grandfather and now, after all his granddaughters and grandsons and nephews and nieces had left to live different lives elsewhere, he had, surprisingly, rediscovered his own.

He got up one morning with a taste of wood and salt in his mouth. A taste that had been long known and filed away by his memory. A father has no time for trifles like boat sailing. He goes out and he provides the best that there is for his family and only when that family is no more is he allowed to hope that he can do so for himself. It is only the way of things.

That morning his life came back to him uncalled for and unattended, maybe out of simple, unexplainable luck that he didn't even particularly deserve. But it is the test of that moment that separates the men who choose to live again, an endeavor perhaps known to be difficult by many of our readers, from those who merely brush away the opportunity as thoughts of... crazy old men.

So Arthur, kind, good ol' Arthur, bought planks, nails, hammers and a wood plane and started work on his life's work. A boat. To cross a mountain. The mountain that sheltered Arthur's village was one of the last to appear on the surface of the world. It was a young, sturdy, healthy mountain, with a pride to match. The storms it took itself to bear were gruesome. Winds that hurled rocks into the air, only to see them blown to dust at the touch of lightning, and avalanches that covered entire forests were matters of the ordinary. But the village had been saved, either out of sympathy or some other form of warm-heartedness that the mountain displayed or, yet again, out of sheer coincidence.

Arthur's boat had to be strong enough to make it through this gauntlet, with him alive and days left to spare. So he worked on his boat. Day and night. And one evening at sunset, he wiped his forehead and put down his hammer and saw that the woodwork was almost done. It was time for him to see the only man that could decide if he had any chance, at all, to survive.

THE BOAT BUILDER FROM THE MOUNTAIN VILLAGE

Part II

'But I want to leave, Phidias. I have to get on the other side of this mountain!' Arthur said, pounding his fist into the table.

'That you must. But you do not have to leave. You have to realize that your place is indeed here, as it always was, what separates who you are now from who you want to be is not a matter of place. It is what you do, not where you do it, and you want to do something impossible and traveling isn't it. You are not going on a journey, you're going to war. You see that, don't you? You just don't know what to call it.'

'But these are just words, Phidias. Will you put your protection charm on my boat? That is all I have to know.'

'We are friends, are we not?'

'We are.'

'Then how could I say no? I will come see the boat tomorrow. Go sleep. Go dream. Go prepare for your war.'

Arthur went and sat himself down on the floor by his bed. As he tapped the wool rug with his fingers, he saw the sharp cliffs of the mountain before him, like a set of giant teeth.

'But I cannot be alone,' he thought. 'I cannot be alone because there is this certainty inside me that I will see the other side of the mountain, just as I live and breathe. There is something which I cannot hear, see or smell that is with me and that will take me there alive. So I know.'

He went to sleep on the floor, with an arm under his head and another covering the tabby cat that had come to be scratched and petted and cared for by its master. And he dreamt that he walked across an entire ocean in his ski boots. Without so much as one of his shoelaces getting wet. And he wondered in his dream about the temperature of the water and if he were to fall in, would his boots drag him down. But he did not. And, as the sun crept up through his window and into his eyes, he reached a golden beach. Then his eyelids parted, and the sand turned into the specks of dust that danced around in a ray of light, scattered about by the cat that was trying to claw its way out of his grasp. There was a knocking on the door and the deep voice of Phidias.

'Arthur! Bring your old sword outside. We will need it.'

So it was as if the charm was already set and the preparations done. The only thing left to do was to push the boat off the pillars. And cross the mountain.

THE BOAT BUILDER FROM THE MOUNTAIN VILLAGE

Part III

The boat sailed and there were no rocks that it did not hit, nor trees that it did not scratch. But it sailed. It floated across the stone, as if carried by the mountain itself. It hovered like a speck in sunlight and it dripped to the top of the mountain swinging and crashing but steadily moving ahead.

On the deck stood Arthur, seasick and lonely and tired from the crashing and murmuring of the trees that cursed at him for ripping and tearing the branches that no mortal had even laid eyes on. And he was torn for being despised and ill willed by all that he encountered and he wondered how this had come to be.

But there was a voice that stayed with him and murmured through the noise. A voice like a memory, like his mother's voice sounded in his mind. Only thinner, and sandier. Like the dry bed of a river that rests under sight, like any absence that stands as proof of something or other.

It was because of the voice that he tied himself to the mast. Where he was seasick no more. Where he saw in all clarity that he was indeed climbing up the mountain in a ship. A ship made of wood and nails, that he had built with his own hands. A ship that had a spell on it, but no stronger than a roof. A ship that stood as the roof of the tallest, proudest mountain in the land, like a raggedy hat on a rich man, that would not come off by hand or scissors or wind.

So when the boat reached the top of the mountain, and tripped across the ledge of the tip and fell like a child on a bumpy country road, the water it raised shot to the sky and rained on Arthur's village and his house and friend Phidias, who then knew he was safe.

Then the water fell and fell, and filled every crack and gap and ditch, and when they were all full, the ocean started pouring from the tip of the mountain, where it had remained hidden, and washed everything in its path to the shore. There it stopped with the village on top of a wave, and its surrounding army of forests on a horde of others. And the village thrived.

Arthur, after having conquered the ego of the mountain that had succumbed before him, became a ship captain, on land. A wayfarer. He traveled the world with Phidias and told stories of his boat. And many others were built, and new heights were reached. Because of one man, who had followed his voice.

Discover new stories at: www.wonderfulroundabout.com

Made in the USA
San Bernardino, CA
14 July 2017